The ANDY K

CATCHING
THE DEPARTED

KULPREET YADAV

tara
India Research Press

The Andy Karan Series
CATCHING THE DEPARTED
Kulpreet Yadav

tara
India Research Press

Flat 6, Khan Market, New Delhi - 110 003
Ph.: 24694610; Fax : 24618637
www.indiaresearchpress.com
contact@indiaresearchpress.com;

2014

ISBN : 978-81-8386-066-6

Printed for India Research Press at Manipal Technologies Limited.

For my brother, Colonel Anil

PROLOGUE

It was a cold night at Tilakpur, a hamlet outside Rewari, seventy kilometres from New Delhi. Dogs barked at low clouds that the wind carried over. At nine, the entire village was asleep. It was quiet, like a school in the dark.

The village wasn't very big. Fifty odd houses huddled together in a disorganized cluster. Lanterns flickered in a few, left to die when the oil ran out. There was no power. Narrow lanes bisected the houses and the smell of supper still lingered in some.

A scooter drove in from the city. It was the only road that connected the hamlet to civilization and to Rewari. This was where the villagers went to sell their crops, buy wedding dresses, or sweets. Or when sick. This was where quacks emptied their pockets. Or paunchy middlemen paid them peanuts for their season-long hardships.

The scooter came to a jerking halt near one of the houses. The man who dismounted couldn't pull it up on its stand. He didn't try the second time and staggered to a door nearby. The scooter slid down behind him, as if in a slow motion before collapsing sideways with a mild thud that resounded through the still silence of the village.

The man knocked at the door, heavily at first and then impatiently. Ten seconds. He began to abuse and started banging the door. He was angry. Four dogs gathered behind him, not barking, cautious, their tails rolling and opening.

The panels in the wooden door parted after a minute. The girl who opened it fell back. The man was too heavy. He couldn't stand any more. She shouted for her mother. Feet came running. The door remained open, moonlight falling through it. The dogs watched them quietly from outside, the movement of their tails halted.

The mother was the first to scream. Her daughter couldn't, though her eyes widened. The man's back was soaked in blood. The mother screamed again. It was a scream of helplessness, sound that carried through the lanes. There was no echo.

She screamed for a whole minute while the daughter stayed petrified, her eyes filled with terror. As if her horror was unyielding.

Slowly, the two women turned him over. Now they were quiet, within hearing distance of each other's breath. It was an effort as the man was tall and heavy — a six feet man who weighed ninety kilos.

He was alive, his face caked with sweat. He coughed and blood spluttered out of his mouth. The woman began to cry. By now her lungs had perhaps recovered from the scream. Then she slapped him as anger took her. How could he return home, drunk and dying?

The girl brought water from the kitchen across the

courtyard. They tried to lift his head, bringing the steel glass close to his trembling lips. He looked at them one last time, that long and caring look, that look which no pain can kill but for a few seconds. Then he slumped in their hands. The head suddenly got heavier and fell from their grip with a clunk on the cemented floor.

The dogs walked away, their heads up as if they were witnessing the dead man's soul rise in the sky. And so did the two men who were hiding, keeping in the shadows, watching the scene anxiously. They had identical bubble-strip sweat on their foreheads. One of them was holding a knife in his hand, blood dripping from its crooked tip.

Two houses away a door opened and a lantern floated out. Soon more doors opened and more lanterns appeared. All the lights converged near the dead man's house and assembled in the courtyard. Minutes later a bike started and roared in the direction from where the scooter had come. The men with the knife were gone.

The dead man was not important to the world. Even in his house, his death brought no sorrow to his family. Yet they mourned. It was a ritual a family couldn't escape in a small village like Tilakpur.

Ladies wailed and the men smoked their *bidis*, their eyes moist — not from the smoke or the cold, but for the family of the dead man. They sat hunched around the corpse, wrapped in shawls and blankets — women on one side, men on the other. Two buffaloes gnawed at the extreme end of the courtyard. They were invisible, their black colour working as stealth. Unless they moved their heads and one of the lights from a *bidi* shone in their eyes and gave them away.

The resident male nurse from the PHC declared the man officially dead an hour later. No more screams followed that, no more wailing either. It was time to plan for tomorrow. But before they did that the villagers began criticizing the dead man in the smaller groups that had formed.

> *He was useless.*
> *He never cared for his family.*
> *He must have had an argument at the bar.*
> *He must have picked a fight somewhere for no reason.*
> *And got killed.*
> *Idiot.*

The cold replaced the shock soon and the shivering began. Neighbours brought in tea and *hookahs*. The *bidis* were crushed on the cemented floor of the courtyard and the pipes grabbed. Blue smoke began to lift above the house, like soiled, crumpled white bed sheets against the moonlit sky.

The police constable arrived at dawn. He hadn't shaved for a week. Villagers smelt alcohol on his breath and cursed him aloud. He abused them back and walked towards the dead man. He shed a tear before the corpse, unlike the others. The dead man was a lawyer and the constable's best friend. He whispered in the dead ear, promised that he would find out who did this. And then he broke down completely. The villagers were surprised to see a real mourner. The dead man's honour in their hearts rose a little.

The funeral was performed. The man was lifted by four stout youngsters. The man's wife and daughter had stayed at home — women weren't allowed at funerals in Tilakpur. Or anywhere else within 500 kilometres, maybe more. They bid him farewell from the door, pale, but vaguely relieved. They were tired.

The firewood caved in the middle as the man was slid on it, but held his weight in the end. The lower logs were stronger. More wood was placed on his body and the log-mesh, with the man in the middle, was consigned to the flames. The man's brother was given this responsibility. A priest who couldn't stop yawning every few minutes chanted prayers. In less than two hours the dead man was reduced to ashes. But by then the villagers had already drifted away.

A shadow had followed them throughout; a shadow that didn't belong to the village; a shadow that didn't come to the village on the motorcycle. This shadow was the last to leave the cremation ground. It walked away, through the mustard fields, towards an obscure horizon in the opposite direction to where the motorcycle had gone.

After thirty minutes the shadow paused in the middle of a field, the village a tiny aberration of blue-black in the distant yellow of the mustard canopy. It turned and flicked a cell phone out. The instrument was tiny. It was enough. Before speaking, the shadow turned. The foggy morning light caught a clean shaven man in a black kurta and pajama, a black bandana on his head. His nose was longer in proportion to his eyes, which were narrow and mean. When he smiled, broken teeth, stained pink from years of betel nut chewing, gaped at nature.

There was a gentle breeze and no sun. It was ten in the morning. The man in black with the broken teeth and crooked nose spoke briefly. Seriously. But when he hung up, he screamed. Mere words floated around, bereft of any meaning. Birds in the distant Acacia trees flew out. He looked like a satisfied man. Someone who had accomplished a big task. He resumed walking away from Tilakpur.

He was still smiling when he dropped face down in the field. The bullet tore through his heart. The big mess that his back became was gobbled by the yellow mustard plants that covered his body in less than a second as he fell.

A motorcycle came to a stop in the distance. *Dhuk, dhuk, dhuk*. Then silence. There were two riders. The driver now eased back on the tilted machine. It was an Enfield Bullet — powerful, macho, mean, 350 cc. A rugged beast with nearly 20 horsepower. The pillion rider waded through the field towards the dead man, a .50 mm bore long distance rifle rocking gently across his shoulder. Barrett M82. Another mean machine, one that could smash anything like an orange on a road by a truck.

The pillion rider brought the body back with him. He was smiling. And so was the dead man whom he threw on the ground face up. The rider was smiling because he had achieved his target. The dead man was smiling because he wasn't aware he had died. He was still happy that he had achieved his target too.

They dug up a deep trench with the shovels they were carrying. The riders could be athletes, or military men. They worked hard and with a sense of urgency. The spot they had chosen was a barren hump where no vegetation grew. It was a bald patch in a field, not more than 20 feet at its extremes. There was no grass on it, encircled though by the lush mustard that now flowed in gentle waves. By the time the men finished it was midday and the sun was getting pesky with the clouds. When it finally won after ten more minutes, they were satisfied that the dead man was buried deep enough for the dogs to dig out.

'I told you it would be easy,' the man who said this was an inch taller than the other. He had brownish hair and a gash on his cheek, like someone had run a blade over it. It showed who was in charge. The shorter man smiled and said, 'It was.'

'Let's collect our reward.' He beamed and lit a cigarette.

The *dhuk, dhuk, dhuk* caught on once again and the motorcycle vanished.

1

Andy Karan was eating a banana, his favourite fruit. Easy to eat, a banana wasn't time consuming. It was healthy too. For someone like him who was always in a hurry, it was a convenient way to stuff up. Sometimes he would eat as many as eight of them, even ten on rare occasions. His personal record was twelve. It had happened just once.

He stood in the balcony of his sixth floor flat in Noida's Sector 25, on the eastern fringe of the capital, New Delhi. Through the light mid-morning fog he could see the outlines of cars parked below. At eight it was cold. He pulled himself indoors as soon as he had finished with the banana.

The phone was ringing in the living room of his two-bedroom flat. He dashed for it. It was Monica, his boss at the *New Delhi Today* magazine. Seven years older than his thirty, she was a demanding boss, but he was used to her.

Monica didn't waste any time with pleasantries. 'Get here, quick!'

This was weird. She needed him for something urgent, but was asking him to come to the office instead. She should have ordered him to rush to the scene of action. That's what journalists are trained to do. You go where the news is happening.

'You mean the office?' Andy hated asking questions, but this time he had little choice.

'You heard me right.' Her voice was edgy and Andy imagined her chewing the end of a pencil which she did whenever nervous. And only twice in the last three years had he seen her biting the pencil. There was silence for two seconds or so, and then he heard the click. She had hung up. Odd.

Andy dropped the idea of eating the second banana. Instead, he collected his items that made his survival kit: cell phone, laptop, wallet, chewing gums, a sweater, a shaving kit. He got out of the house and waited in front of the lift. His patience ran out in five seconds and he rushed down the stairs.

Though the sun was yet to emerge from under the thick blanket of fog, the diffused daylight caught his face.

Andy was a handsome man, five feet ten, whose face had retained its boyish charm. His light brown hair was short, almost like a crew cut, and his eyes were like river pebbles high in the mountains, clear and cold.

In thirty minutes he was at the office. Monica was still chewing the pencil. She started straightaway without looking at him.

'Last year around this time, a man was murdered at Tilakpur. It's a small village near Rewari. His name was Ram Avtar.'

Monica looked up and Karan thought she looked tired. There were red rings around the edges of her eyes and her face had an ashen tinge. He heard her without hearing her, as she paused to examine the damage she had done to the pencil. Perhaps realizing that it was now getting out of control, she kept the pencil at the farthest distance from her on the table, and continued, 'According to my sources in intelligence, he may have been killed because he knew too much. Perhaps, he had some information, may be even about a terror plot...' She stared hard at the pencil, resisting the temptation and resumed, 'Ram Avtar was a drunkard, no one seemed to care much about him, but he was killed. May be he spoke to some friends? I want you to head straight there and check out if there's a story.'

Andy was disappointed. He had hoped for more concrete information. But she appeared to be desperately clutching at straws to stay afloat. She was all over the place, she was worried about something. It was fine with him.

He looked at Monica. The despair couldn't rob her of her beauty. Her brown eyes were big and expressive. The shoulder length hair curled inwards, desperately trying to reach her cleavage, and the lips were turgid. Monica had been a successful model till ten years ago and it was written all over her. Her mannerisms were impeccable, like fresh out of a finishing school. But this morning she seemed shaken.

She looked up with raised eyebrows, making him realize that she knew he was staring at her. Andy flashed a lame smile and said he would head for Tilakpur straightaway.

He walked out of the office. Connaught Place was noisy, but vibrant at ten in the morning. The sky was a clear blue by now and a hesitant sun had warmed things a bit. Andy's orders were to leave immediately, so he walked with long strides and reached his car. His mind was abuzz with all the possible options. He liked this part, and it was precisely why he had become an investigative journalist. Five years in the Indian Army and Andy was always hungry for adventure, for the thrills. Life in the Army was an adrenalin rush and he knew that an investigative reporter's was no less. But there was a difference. Of course, in the Army there was a clear definition of the enemy, but in journalism everyone was a friend and yet a potential enemy. The enemy coexisted with friends, right amidst them.

He turned the ignition of his Maruti Swift and joined the traffic on the outer circle of Connaught Place. He turned into Kasturba Gandhi Marg and hit the road that encircled India Gate. Switching from Akbar Road to Teen Murti, he crossed several bungalows where ministers, senior bureaucrats and judges still slept as he reached Shanti Path. On both his sides were embassies, flowers and greens in the foreground. He glanced at the US Embassy on his right, Japan and Pakistan on his left and several others, before joining National Highway 8 via RK Puram, with its cage-like government quarters scattered all around, small windows in all of them. In these he knew lived those who worked for the bungalow inhabitants he had crossed minutes earlier.

An aircraft descended overhead as he drove westwards towards Rewari, the sun right behind him. It felt hot and he was hungry. The only banana that he had eaten was all burnt up by this time and he needed more calories. He made a mental note to eat before heading out to Tilakpur, where finding a restaurant seemed unlikely.

His plan was simple: speak to the family of the murdered man, look around, ask questions to a few more, leave his telephone number, and throw a few scares to make the wrong people a little uneasy. He hoped for the suspects to show up.

Andy decided to stay for the night at a hotel at Rewari. Monica wouldn't fuss over the bill as the case seemed important. He'd decide on the rest of the plan the next day. She had given him two more names — friends of the dead man. One was a constable and the other, a bartender.

Monica had also said his Army training would come in handy this time, more than the other cases he had handled in the past three years. Army training in a village in Haryana? He just smiled at her.

To his left and right, the Gurgaon skyline screamed for attention and as always he couldn't resist admiring the buildings. A colossal amount of cement, glass and steel had been amalgamated to form interesting shapes, painted with bright colours. Logos of famous brands mocked at him, almost giggling at his inability to avoid staring at them. He kept his eyes on the road with difficulty.

But in less than half an hour it was all over. Now he crossed villages, which were trying to masquerade as mini towns. They had almost overflowed on to the road. Tractors, bullocks, camels, cars, SUVs and cycles coexisted on the highway. Trucks moved alongside his car like snails in slow-motion. Andy struggled to drive with consistent speed, having to change gears furiously at regular intervals.

Just before entering Rewari City, he stopped for a bite at a wayside *dhaba*. *Aloo paratha*, curd and radish salad. Everything was made fresh and he loved savouring it seated outside on an airy cot, the popular Indian charpoy. In forty minutes he was back on the road and consulted the GPS on his phone. The road to Tilakpur turned before Rewari City and Andy slipped in as it appeared.

When he finally drove into Tilakpur, the village seemed empty. Mid-afternoon, he mused. Leaving his car at the edge of the village under the shade of a banyan tree, the base of which was caught in a cemented structure about eight feet in diameter and three feet in height, he slowly walked into the village.

Ram Avtar's house was smaller than the others and easy to locate. He just had to ask directions from one person. He wondered if it was a good idea to knock –one of those uneasy moments in the daily life of an investigative reporter. In the end he knocked at the wooden door with a loosely flexed wrist. The sound seemed to echo inside the wood as if it had been hollowed by termites. After a minute the door was opened by a middle-aged woman. She could be Ram Avtar's widow.

Andy folded his hands into a Namaste and smiled. When her eyebrows started to rise, he asked his first question.

'Ram Avtar's house?'

She nodded and stood blocking the door.

'I know he is not around any more, but can I ask you something?'

'If you are here to collect the money he borrowed from you, I'll tell you right now that he never told me about his financial dealings.' She began to close the door, but Andy was quicker in responding.

'No, he never took any money from me. In fact, I never met him.' The inward swing of the wooden panels stopped halfway and she stared at him blankly. He guessed her state of mind. If he hadn't met her husband, what could he possibly want?

'So what do you want from us?' Her question confirmed it.

'I just want to ask you a few questions.'

'Why?' Her eyes narrowed now and Andy was not sure how much more time he had before she closed the door on him. If she did that his chances of making any further enquiry would be lost forever.

'Please don't get alarmed. I'm a journalist. I learnt he was killed and I wanted to do a story, so that such incidents don't happen in the future.'

'Yes, he was killed. He was my family's breadwinner. Now all the money has dried up. There is nothing more for me to say.' She closed the door. Andy thanked the closed door and walked away.

Like all village women, Ram Avtar's wife had the pride which comes living with bare minimum needs and surrounded by nature. The ambition of such people is never too high. There are no comparisons to make. The daily needs of food are fulfilled by the farmland and cattle at home. Unlike other parts of the country, in Haryana there is no dearth of food.

Andy walked through the crisscross of narrow passages between the houses. Evening was approaching fast and he knew he didn't have more than an hour before it was completely dark. He came across an abandoned well in the centre of the village. Perhaps this was the source of water till a few years ago. He could see the water pipelines going in and out of the houses now.

A man sat on the steps leading to the well. His head hung low and Andy wasn't sure if the man was in a contemplative mood, or if he was just killing time. Two boys, about ten years old, played nearby with hockey sticks and a red plastic ball. There was no one else in sight.

When Andy came to a halt near the man, it was perhaps his feet that the man noticed first. He got up immediately and smiled. A rare gesture.

'I am new here.'

The man didn't answer but walked away, his expression uncertain. Andy called out behind him, but the man didn't stop. He vanished behind a house at the end of the narrow passage. The boys didn't stop their game. For them scoring a goal had a higher priority. Andy stood for a while out of child-like curiosity. The boys were sweating, though it was very cold. Their task was to defend their territory — the goal posts that were marked by their *chappals* kept apart.

Andy watched them play for fifteen more minutes, till one of them caught his eyes and stopped. He walked up to Andy and smiled.

'What's your name?'

'Suresh.' His two front teeth were missing.

'You play well.' Andy smiled and that sent him back to the game.

Andy walked back to his car. But this time he crossed a few people who were walking their buffaloes home, carelessly swinging the sticks that they held firmly in their hands. The buffaloes were wet and he could tell by the green grime that sat on the edges of their stomachs that they were on their way home after a dip in the village pond. At home, the green sheen would be washed off with a water hose. No one took special notice of him.

But when he was about to get into the car, he heard a man clear his throat right behind him. Andy turned and was face to face with a tall man. Andy didn't like him at all. The man had an air of authority — something that comes easily to those who want more from the world around them. People who are greedy and ambitious. Though he didn't like him, he was hoping this man would provide him a lead.

'Who are you?' The man's accent was weird, as if he was trying to speak in an artificial voice.

Andy replied that he had lost his way.

'But Ram Avtar's wife said you are a journalist.'

'Oh, yes. I do freelance journalism too.' News in Tilakpur travelled fast, he thought. This was weird.

'And you knew her husband had died.'

'Yes, I'm hoping to write an article on the dead man.' Andy's irritation showed, and he wanted it that way. He opened the door of the car to get inside. The man pushed the door closed.

'I am talking to you!'

The man had taken the bait and he now seemed angry.

'Who killed him? Was it you?' Andy glared at him this time, infuriating the man. The man was surprised, but only for a moment and then his anger started to rise.

'If it was you or any of your friends, then you're in big trouble!' Andy didn't wait for the man to reply. He sat down in the car and drove away, the man breathing like a wild animal behind him.

He wanted to ruffle the village a bit. He wanted all the dust that had settled to lift a little. And he knew when that happened the guilty would start becoming uncomfortable.

But who would kill a useless drunk like Ram Avtar,

one who was penniless too? Then why was he killed? Did he really have information about terrorists planning an attack? It seemed improbable, as no attacks had happened anywhere in the country for the last one year. Monica had also said his post-mortem was not done. Something was not right. Andy needed to get to work.

2

Monica stared at the closed door of her office for a long time after Andy Karan left. She wasn't sure if she had done the right thing by sending him to Tilakpur. But she had little choice.

Running the *New Delhi Today* magazine was Monica's responsibility. The owner, when he appointed her, had explained that the subscription of the magazine should continually rise. He wasn't interested in generating revenue from advertisements, or who she selected to cover her stories. His interest was limited to the progressive growth of the magazine's popularity. He wanted to achieve a very large reader base and had continued to set very stringent six-monthly targets for Monica.

She recalled his final warning. 'If the readership growth rate drops, consider yourself fired. I don't care what you do, I just want readers to be pulled to my magazine like moths to a flame.'

He had gone on to tell her that he didn't care about ethics or morality in her discharging her duties, as long as readers multiplied over time.

Monica had hired a statistician-cum-webmaster who kept a tab on the number of subscribers and visitors. A week ago, he had come to her office with a long, dull face. He informed her that in the absence of a new spark, the numbers might level out soon. After which, in the continued absence of a new and juicy story, the subscriber figures would begin to drop. These were desperate times and her survival depended on it. She was almost at the tipping point.

Her first thoughts were of Andy. Her source was genuine. An old friend. They had worked together earlier as well. There was no need for Monica to doubt the story. Something big was going on at Tilakpur. A man was already dead. She was the only person who knew about this so far. She needed to use this to her advantage.

Initially, she had been reluctant about sending Andy Karan. Over the last three years of working with him, Monica had begun to like Andy. He was polite and disciplined, and in a strange way, she felt very comfortable around him. She didn't know what her feelings for him were, but she was certain that she didn't want to send him into the eye of the storm.

Yet, in the end, to keep her job that she desperately needed, she had asked him to go to Tilakpur. There was no one else who could get the job done more thoroughly. She had to choose between her job and Andy. And she had chosen the job. At least for now.

And now she was worried like hell. The informer had also warned her that there was danger in trying to uncover the information. Danger to life.

She sat alone for a long time in the office, unaware of the fact that she had missed her lunch and night had fallen outside. She imagined Andy moving about in the village, not fully aware of the dangers that awaited him. She did warn him, but was she explicit enough? Monica had no way of knowing. When finally she did get up to leave, she folded her hands and said a silent prayer. Something didn't feel right, but there was nothing she could do at the moment.

Andy walked into a dingy little moss-encrusted building just opposite the bus stand in the middle of the city. The neon sign outside blinked, "Hot—", the E and the L were not working. He was certain that this hotel would easily suit his requirements and budget. He checked-in just after sunset and walked through the cold corridors to get to his room. The room was small, but cleaner than he had hoped. The Nepali boy who showed him in smiled and said, 'Hot water through tap only in the morning. If you want now, I bring.'

Andy said he was fine and the boy walked away, closing the door softly behind him. The room had a window through which he could see the street below. The street was well lit and scooters and cars honked endlessly. In the distance he could see buses parked at an angle, their heads touching the platform where men and women bathed in milky white light, sat hunched.

He unpacked. The shaving kit went into the bathroom where the smell of soap still remained from the previous occupant. The mirror on the wash basin was like a medicine cabinet. He opened it to keep the shaving kit inside. There was a condom kept there. Was it placed on purpose? So that the occupant asked for the service?

There was a convector heater in the room which the boy had switched on before leaving. Now, its filament glowed a bright red. Andy checked the time. At seven it was too early to think about dinner. The room had warmed up by now and he removed his jacket. His plan was to meet the police constable first thing tomorrow. Right now, it was the perfect opportunity for him to meet the barman.

Andy washed his face and hands. The water was freezing, but he felt refreshed after the cold was absorbed by his skin. The towel smelt peculiar so he dried his hands on his handkerchief. There was a knock. The door didn't have a peephole, he realized. He paused and wondered if it was safe to open.

Andy wasn't expecting anyone. Usually if a guest took longer to open, the hotel staff would announce it was them. But there was pin drop silence outside. Which meant whoever knocked was certainly not the hotel staff.

He got up and stood near the door, his ears straining for any sound. Silence. So far he hadn't made any real enemies and therefore had nothing to fear. Unless his visit to the village had been taken seriously. Monica had asked him to be careful. On a hunch he decided to wait for the second knock. Minutes ticked. There was no sound. After about five minutes he opened the door slowly, inch by inch. There was no one outside. He closed it again.

Did he imagine the knock? He called the reception from the intercom kept on the bedside table.

'No, Sir. It wasn't us.'

Ten minutes later Andy came out of his room, locked the door and walked towards the stairs on light feet. There were six rooms on either side of the corridor, and except his, only two others seemed occupied. He crossed the one on his right that had a television turned on inside and Hindi film songs played at high volume. He could see the light under the door of the last room to his left. No sound came from this room.

The receptionist was replaced by the Nepali boy who sat pretending to scratch the stubble that he didn't have. He was no more than 16 years, though he thought of himself as 20. Andy smiled and asked him the way to the Blue Soda bar. The enquiry seemed to excite the boy. He said his name was Ramu.

It was a ten minute walk through air full of dust and horns. Stray goats and cows wandered on the roads as did vehicles and people. Andy was careful to see if he was being followed. Just in case. But he wasn't. Whoever knocked at his door wasn't at his heels.

The Blue Soda bar was a poorly-lit small room at the back of a hotel. The hotel was similar to where Andy stayed and he wondered if it was better for him to shift here. There were ten tables scattered on a floor that was dark, each with four upright chairs, their backs so close that the chairs touched. The light inside took some time getting used to, after which Andy walked to a table and sat down. There were no stools to sit on and there was no bar counter. Small town bars always looked the same. Tables and chairs in a room, like a restaurant that also served liquor, and where women were rarely seen.

Five of the tables were occupied, enveloped in cigarette smoke. Music from old Hindi films blared from the speakers. Andy thought the male voice sounded like a female's trying to be husky. His best guess was that the speakers seemed to have fallen out with reality and were perforated with overuse. Or by ants and termites that perhaps frolicked in them.

No one must have noticed him as nothing moved for

about five minutes while he got used to his surroundings. Finally, an elderly waiter appeared by his side and asked what he wanted. He ordered Old Monk, his favourite from the Army days. A glass that felt slippery to touch was brought by the waiter, along with a complimentary bowl of peanuts. He thanked him and wondered if it was all right to engage him in a conversation. Perhaps later, he decided. The waiter walked away. From what he could see there were no more waiters in the bar. Sitting there sipping his drink, Andy sent Monica a message asking for more information.

The waiter hung on for a few seconds longer after Andy had three drinks. It was obvious that he wanted to be nice and chatty with him. All for a tip. He knew their methods. Small towns or Delhi, the bar waiters were always the same — greedy and predictable.

Andy grabbed the opportunity and asked him, 'This is a good bar. I like the atmosphere here.'

It was a wrong start as the waiter walked away after giving him a long, cold stare. Perhaps the lie was too obvious. The bar wasn't the kind that big city guys like him were expected to appreciate. Maybe all the others before him might have complained and therefore the man was surprised, perhaps irritated. Andy kicked himself.

He asked for a refill and a plate of chilli chicken that the waiter recommended. Andy saw him soften as he slipped a crumpled hundred rupee note in his hand. The elderly waiter suddenly lit up and Andy's status climbed higher. In no time he was jumping all around him, taking extra care, bringing plates, cleaner glasses, paper napkins, asking him if he wanted to listen to any particular song. Andy played it cool and said the songs were fine.

Two more tables were occupied as a few more men walked in. Through the stench of stale peanuts, burnt out cigarettes and heavy liquor, Andy thought he recognized one of the men in a group of three. He appeared to be the same person Andy had met and confronted just before leaving Tilakpur. But he wasn't one hundred percent sure due to the darkness and the smoky haze all around him. Andy knew he had to move fast.

'I want to meet Rohtas,' he finally asked the waiter.

'Rohtas called earlier in the evening to inform us that he wasn't well.'

The waiter said he would be happy to give him Rohtas' address if Andy was desperate to meet him. Andy declined the offer. Monica had sent some more info. Rohtas, the bar man, who was the dead Ram Avtar's friend, was 30 years old and lived close to the bus stop. Her text ended with an address and a message. 'Be careful'. He imagined her big eyes filled with concern, while his brain played a flashback of Monica over the years, their age difference. Seven years, Andy, seven years! Andy had always been women's favourite, something that gave him the upper hand in a relationship. But now was not the time to think about women.

Based on the information shared by Monica, Rohtas was very close to Andy's hotel. He paid the bill, left a generous tip of another hundred and walked out, without looking at the man he suspected was from Tilakpur. This time Andy was followed and he spotted the tail in no time. Andy spotted a few vegetable vendors winding up their make-shift shops for the day and he used the scant crowd to his advantage. When the tail was out of sight for a few seconds, he ran into a narrow alley that appeared to his left and took two left turns to come out right behind the tail. He hid at the back of a small kiosk and watched the man look left and right, wondering where he had disappeared. After a minute he was joined by another man. Now bathed in the street light Andy identified the man from Tilakpur. It meant that the man was at the bar too. His hunch was right. Perhaps he even knew where he lived. This was not a good sign.

But had he known where Andy lived he wouldn't bother following him. Or maybe he was being followed not to find where he lived, but to see where he went. He thought of the knock at his door once again. Was it a warning?

Andy watched them standing under the street light and speaking to each other. They seemed comfortable, but amateurish, not bothered to stay in the shadows. Or maybe they were not scared of him? Perhaps after getting away with things for far too long, they had just stopped worrying about themselves! They seemed to be in control, like people in power who called the shots.

The two men walked away after five more minutes, in the direction opposite to where his hotel was. Andy got out of his hiding spot and reached his hotel within a few minutes. The Nepali boy looked at him and smiled, his eyes droopy. He looked tired and turned his attention to the television, where the climax was unfolding in an old Hindi film. It seemed intense. There was a woman dancing and there were people with guns blazing around her. If the director of the movie was to walk in at this moment and see the effect of his climax on a viewer, he would die of a heart attack.

Andy sat down on the sofa near the entrance. The Nepali boy was snoring by the time the hero rescued the woman and killed the villain. He got up and switched the television off. The silence was deafening. At ten at night there were no more vehicles on the road. People slept early in small towns and Andy found the streets deserted on his way back to the hotel. He waited for any movement or sound that wasn't ordinary. There was none.

Andy shook his head. He was taking the instances too seriously. He had done nothing so far, except asking a lady how her husband died and slightly annoying a village buffoon. But there would be dangers ahead. It excited him. Danger always excited him. Where life and death became part of a plan, Andy Karan felt most comfortable.

He took the stairs to the first floor. The corridor felt colder, or perhaps his senses were just heightened. The same rooms were occupied. One was quiet, while music from the television played on in the other. He stood for a few seconds in front of his room, looking left and right. There was nothing unusual. He turned the key and walked in.

Suddenly, a shadow leapt at him and he felt something hit hard on his head. And then it was all dark.

3

When Andy opened his eyes all he could see was white. He tried to turn his head, but couldn't. He realized that he was looking at the ceiling of a room. The ceiling was extra white, with Plaster of Paris cornices in the ends. It meant he was neither at the village, nor somewhere else in captivity. Kidnappers never kept their targets in brilliantly lit rooms with tasteful ceilings.

He tried to move his hands. Relief. He lifted one hand and then the other and saw them with his own eyes. He then tried to move his toes and was successful in that too. He closed his eyes and tried to feel the pain. Except the heaviness in his head, he felt nothing else.

'Doctor, doctor! Please come fast... He is conscious now!' Monica's voice, concerned and urgent, but he couldn't see her. So he was at a hospital in Delhi. The relief was so enormous that without realizing he slipped back into a deep sleep

When he opened his eyes next, the ceiling was darker. Perhaps it was night and the lights had been turned down to a minimum. His head was still stiff. He tried to speak. If there was an attendant in the room, he wanted him to know that he was awake.

A nurse's face appeared. Seeing her in her white uniform, Andy felt like he was looking at an angel. She smiled and gave him all the information he needed. He was at the Safdarjung Hospital in Delhi. He had a concussion due to a head injury. But there was nothing to worry about as he was responding well to the medicines and treatment.

'Who brought me here?' he asked.

'A lady called Monica. She said she's your colleague.'

'She's my boss. Is she here?'

'No. It's four o'clock now... in the morning. She left at nine, informing me that she'd return in the morning. Please rest now... you shouldn't exert yourself like this.'

'I feel fine.'

'Please try to sleep.' Andy saw her face disappear and the dark ceiling was all he could see after she was gone.

He closed his eyes and was taken back to the moment which started it all. He had not noticed the signals properly.

The Nepali boy couldn't have fallen asleep at ten, that too at the reception itself, not unless someone wanted exactly that to happen. The boy had been sedated. It was foolish of him to be bothered about conditions outside the room rather than inside. Perhaps he was losing his edge, not getting enough such cases to keep his alertness intact.

But he was alive. This meant either the attackers were kind, or they didn't intend to kill him. It had to be the second. The attackers were professionals. They knew exactly where he stayed. They got to him when he was most vulnerable. And knocked him out with a precision strike, ensuring he didn't sustain any major injury. Only professionals could achieve such finesse. They were sending him a message: 'Look, we could have killed you, but we spared your life instead.' Andy could almost hear them. Their threat hung in the air, forcing Andy to now take note of them.

His attackers obviously didn't like his asking the dead man's wife about her husband. They didn't want him at the village. And they didn't want him to meet Rohtas, the barman. They wanted him to stay away. They expected him to be frightened.

But in doing so, they left the biggest message — they had something to hide from the world. Andy smiled just as the window in his room began to turn translucent. Day was breaking outside the Safdarjung Hospital and Andy was happy to find his capacity to think intact.

He wanted to go back to Rewari this very moment and shout at them that he wasn't scared. He was an ex-Army officer. And even after a soldier stops wearing the uniform, he still remains a soldier. They were challenging his basic training, his existence and his intent to find the truth. But he was not someone who could be frightened easily.

The heaviness in his head was back. Andy realized that to do anything, he first had to get well. He closed his eyes and decided to wait for Monica, hoping to get some sleep till then.

When he heard Monica's voice, she was lightly shaking his shoulder. He opened his eyes and smiled at her. Just looking at her large eyes staring at him with concern made him feel a lot better.

'I told you to be careful, Andy.' Just like Monica, always on the edge, always predictable.

'Sorry.'

'No, I am. I should have...' her voice trailed off as she turned her head left and right to see if anyone was within hearing distance. He was right all along. She had been hiding something.

There was a long, eerie pause as Andy looked at her. She looked beautiful, but her moist, concerned eyes revealed her lack of sleep. Her cheeks were red with exhaustion and she wore no makeup. Andy was surprised. This was the first time he had seen Monica without makeup.

'Why didn't you tell me everything?'

'I couldn't. You have to trust me.' Her voice was sharp, and still defiant.

'Fair enough!'

'Andy I know this is not fair, so please don't make it worse for me. I wouldn't do this to you. People like you are rare... people who protect the truth, people who have no pretentions, no expectations, no political gains and no interest in money.'

This morning she was excessively emotional too. Andy had never seen her like this in the last three years of having known her and meeting her almost daily. First it was the pressure — he remembered the pencil — and now she was on the verge of breaking down. He stayed quiet.

'I don't want you to go there any more. The doctor says you will be fine in a couple of days. Once you're discharged, I want you to go home, send me your resignation letter and stay at home. Find yourself another job...I will help you find one, that's a promise!'

'But I want to go back there. I can't leave the case halfway. It's unethical!'

She laughed. 'Unethical? This word exists only in the dictionary of you Armywallas.'

Andy was disappointed. He had always admired Monica

for her passion and integrity and he respected her for it. But she was behaving strangely now. This was not the Monica he knew.

A doctor came in for the morning rounds. The nurse in his tow answered his questions, while Andy and Monica waited. After they were gone, Andy asked, 'Where did you find me?'

'Near Mahipalpur. I got a call at midnight from an unknown guy the day before yesterday. He found you were lying on the road, bleeding. I brought you straight here. The doctors said another two hours and it would have been too late.'

'Thanks for that...Say, where's my car?' Andy was careful not to agitate her any further, but he wanted to know the facts.

'It was right next to where I found you. I think the attackers brought you to Delhi in your own car. There was blood all over the back seat. I got it cleaned so that it doesn't remind you of anything.'

'What did the police say?'

'They haven't been able to make much headway yet. They should be here any moment to record your statement. I think it will be best if you don't talk about this assignment.'

'Why? I'd like to speak the truth.' Andy was losing patience. He did not like his own tone, but he couldn't control himself either.

'Andy please, for your own life's sake!'

'Monica, I want you to understand that I don't believe in giving up. I will go right back in there and find out what they're hiding from the world.'

Monica didn't speak for long. Then she slowly got up, wished him a speedy recovery and walked away. Andy heard the clank of the keys on the metal table on his bedside. She had left him his car keys. Then it was quiet once again and he was all alone.

He lied to the police in the end. It was late afternoon when they arrived — two fat inspectors, their paunches well ahead of them. Their breath had whisky from last night and their accent was a typical Haryanvi. He thought they looked like cops from the movies, not from real life. Speaking the truth would only make matters worse for himself. The less they knew, the better off he would be.

'Who attacked you?' asked one. The other yawned.

'I don't know. Something hit me from behind.'

'Where were you?' Now the one who asked the question yawned.

'I was visiting a friend at Rewari.'

'Do you have any enemies?' No one yawned this time.

'No.'

'The heavy thing that hit you from behind, was it brought down on your head by a human or was it something like a tree branch that fell as you walked on?'

'I have no idea. It could have been absolutely anything.'

'OK. We know where you work. If you have any other information please call us. Unless we know more we can do nothing. You understand?' He gave his number. They were gone faster than they had come. But the faint smell of hung-over whisky remained.

The attacker's plan had worked well for them so far. Not injuring him grievously was a two-pronged strategy: One, the police won't have enough to commit time and resources, and two, the attacked person would stay away fearing for his life.

No one visited Andy in the next two days. He felt lonely and bored. He wished he had a girlfriend. She would have been there with him, taking care, keeping his spirits up. But he wasn't fortunate enough to fall in love with anyone so far. Earlier in the Army, he never had the opportunity. As a young officer, he worked mostly in difficult, desolate areas. And now as an investigative journalist he hobnobbed only with criminals and thugs. He didn't have to work very hard to get laid, thanks to the two acquaintances he had. They were still expecting him to fall in love, but all he wanted from them was their body and its fluids. He was almost tempted to call them to the hospital, but refrained when he realized how they'd get the wrong signals about their relationship.

The day he was discharged from the hospital, the doctor explained how a head injury needed to be watched for as long as a year. Things could go out of hand. He had to be careful. The warning signs were explained to him and he made a mental note.

Andy walked out feeling as healthy as before, and soon located his car in the parking lot. The back seat was clean and it smelt nice, like just after a servicing. He wished Monica hadn't done this. Perhaps he could have found some clues. But now it was all washed clean.

He drove to the toll plaza that majestically stood between Gurgaon and Delhi, a restless cluster of vehicles aiming to break through to the other side. The attackers must have driven through it with him in the back seat, unconscious and defenceless. He pulled up on one side, walked across to the office at the end and asked for the video tapes.

The staff looked uncertain. Andy flashed his card. The manager said they only stored data for three days. He walked back to his car and turned back towards Delhi. He spotted a small diner along the highway and pulled in to eat something. There was nothing to celebrate, except that he was alive. He ordered chicken biryani and beer. Satiated, he drove to Connaught Place and asked for Monica at the office reception. She was alarmed to see him, but only for a second. Shock soon changed to happiness and she asked him to come in at once. He sat across her in the cabin. Monica started by asking how he felt.

'Better than before.'

She smiled and paused to order two cups of tea over the intercom, without even asking if he wanted one. Andy didn't disagree.

'I didn't tell the Police everything...thought you should know.'

'What did you tell them?'

'I said I was visiting a friend at Rewari when something hit my head. They weren't suspicious. People throw all sorts of things from windows in our country, so I guess they just assumed this to be one such case. One of them left me his number.'

'Hmmm...'

The tea arrived and they sipped it in silence. Then Andy said, 'Monica, I'm going after them, whether or not you assign me this case. I just want you to know that.'

She said she understood, her voice just a whisper. After tea, she suddenly declared she had work to do. Andy walked away, but turned to look over his shoulder once, before exiting through the main door. He had crossed several waist high cubicles. Clerks and copywriters worked endlessly in them. Monica was exactly where he had expected her, peeping out of her cabin. Their eyes met, but she ducked inside in a flash.

Andy smiled and walked out. He knew he had no friends in the police and perhaps none in the company he worked. It wasn't a pleasant discovery, but he wasn't bothered.

Perhaps for the millionth time, he thought about the appropriateness of his name Karan, which he used as his last name. Andy Karan was born Anil Karan Singh. He was a love child. His father never married his mother and he never saw him. His mother was a florist and she decided not to marry anyone after being deserted by the man she truly loved. She died when he was twelve and he couldn't remember much of her. Except snatches of memories that haunted him every now and then.

His mother had once told him, a few months before her death, 'I named you Anil when you were born, after the Sun God. I thought you looked as bright as the sun when I held you in my arms for the first time. But on the same day, your father abandoned me. I cried for days, months, and added Karan to your name. I know you will grow to become a fine human being, but you might fail at every juncture due to me, a woman who brought you into the world without a marriage. Your future is doomed because of my sins.' She choked while saying this and

Andy, as a young boy, thought his mother was dying. He cried with her for a long, long time.

A month after his mother's death, at her sister's house who took Andy in, Andy bought a copy of the Mahabharata and read it during the nights. He read the complete epic and re-read the chapters about Karan several times over. Like him, the Karan of the Mahabharata was an illegitimate child. He was surprised how a brave and principled man, one so kind and generous, was killed by others to serve their own means. Andy didn't like the idea of staying with the name, but something inside always stopped him from removing it.

He stopped outside the office and opened his wallet from which he removed the picture of his mother. She was young when it was taken and was smiling at the camera. He couldn't tell when the picture was taken, but she seemed like a young mother, full of hope for the world and her child, her creation. How much he missed his mother. He wanted to shed a tear, but like always, he couldn't. Men never cry, his Army trainers had taught him.

4

There was a man standing right next to Andy's car. He didn't know him. Andy put his guard up, alert after what had already happened to him at Rewari. As Andy was approaching the car, the man slowly walked up to him and asked for directions to the local market. Andy played on and pointed a finger to his left. It was a silly question to ask as they were already at the market. The man thanked him and shook his hand. He slipped in a piece of paper into his palm. Then the man was gone. Andy knew the man was a one-time messenger and he wouldn't see him again in his life.

Andy slid into the driver's seat and sat still for a moment. He turned his head an entire 360 degrees to make sure that no one was watching him and satisfied, Andy unfolded the paper. The A4 sheet had been folded several times to make it small enough to hide within one's palm.

It was a hand-drawn map. Delhi. Andy followed the roads scribbled along the map — a bridge on Ring Road just beyond a dull logo of the Hyatt, the lack of proportion making it somewhat difficult for Andy to decipher. Under the logo was an arrow, which could only point towards the Sarojini Nagar Market. On the edge of the market was a glass which quite obviously signified a juice shop. Andy studied the brief legends on the map and understood which particular juice shop he was expected at. At the bottom of the map were six numbers. Though spread over two lines, Andy could easily make them out.

20

2030

20th December. The meeting was scheduled for this evening, at eight thirty in the evening. Andy had a lot of time to kill before that. He pushed the crumpled paper deep into his pocket and started the car.

It was dusk and the fog hung like a promise of what lay ahead — a cold evening. He drove to his house, opened the main door and walked into a dark room. There was no one. He knew it. The lock had not been tampered with and there was no other way anyone could enter his house without being seen. There was only one balcony and it faced a twelve-floored building with old people living in it. Old people who sat in their balconies all day long and who had all the time to watch the world around them.

He turned on the lights and the drawing room, with its sparse furniture, woke into existence. He placed his shoulder bag with his laptop and other items on the sofa and sunk into it himself, recollecting the morning's events.

Andy had never told anyone at the *New Delhi Today* magazine, not even Monica, about his little agreement with Army Intelligence. The truth was he himself wasn't very sure about his role there. He was also under oath. So there was no guilt. In any case, his employment status was only when needed. And it was the second time he had been ushered in like this for a meeting. The first one, a year ago, turned out to be a practice run. He had been told that had he not reached the designated spot on time, they would have struck him off the list. Maybe he'd be fine with it if they did indeed do that. Except that the government would not have contacted him for any espionage work in the future. Andy heaved a sigh of relief for passing the test. Deep down, he loved doing this once in a while still.

So, he was on. But for what? It was just after six. He switched on the geyser in the bathroom and sat in front of television browsing news channels. After five minutes, when he realized nothing sensational had happened to the world around him, he skipped channels till he reached the Movies package of his DTH operator.

Andy loved watching movies, particularly the Hollywood ones. Hindi movies were usually tear jerkers with an abundance of loud colour, make-up and songs. He didn't like them very much. There were exceptions, of course, and once in a while if a friend gave a positive feedback about a Hindi movie, he would go and watch it at the theatre. His main interest still remained with English movies, with their speed, violence and bad people who invariably got their just desserts, however smart or strong they looked at the beginning of the film. It was believable.

Andy let the TV play on silently, while he walked into the loo. He took a long, leisurely hot shower, allowing the warm water to fall on his back. He felt alive and it made him love life more dearly. As the water turned cold, he turned off the knob and stepped out. He dried himself and put on his clothes quickly.

Traffic on the road at seven was bad. He crawled through Sector 18, with its signature malls on both sides and took the expressway to reach the DND toll way. By five minutes to eight he had parked his car and located the juice shop. About a dozen people milled around, asking for their drinks, some sipping them quietly not too far from the counter. A fat man took the money and a thin man handed out the drinks.

He stood there uncertain, wondering if he should move around or order some juice while he waited. The people who wanted to meet him knew exactly where he was and how he looked. But he didn't know them. So the onus to make the first move was theirs, not his.

After fifteen minutes, he ordered a sweet lime juice. The thin man handed him a Styrofoam glass. He carried it a little further and stood under a mango tree. Whoever was there to meet him must be watching and would appreciate his presence of mind to stand at a relatively secluded spot.

As if in answer to Andy's actions, an old man walked up to him and asked where the *paan* shop was. Andy said he didn't know and the old man walked away. No one had still showed up and it was already eight thirty. Andy was wondering what to do when the same old man returned. He said he was still trying to figure out where the *paan* shop was.

'I really don't know where it is.'

'I don't want to know where it is.'

'So?'

'Meet me at Diva. It's a restaurant in GK II, in the M Block market. Nine, sharp.'

And then the old man was gone, as mysteriously as he had arrived. Andy felt cheated. He wasn't someone they had to take so many precautions with. They could meet him anywhere — including his house. Why this cat and mouse game?

Not sure what to do next, Andy decided to drive back to Greater Kailash II. He was quite irritated when he walked into the restaurant. The time was a few minutes before nine. He didn't look around and sat down at the nearest table. Within seconds the old man slid in front of him. He smiled and Andy responded to his expression feebly.

'Who sent you to Tilakpur?' The old man didn't believe in wasting time.

'My magazine.' Andy too didn't bother to indulge in any pleasantries.

'After what happened to you, they may not be willing to take more risks. But I want you to go back there.'

The old man paused to order wine, Shiraz Cabernet by Jacob's Creek. Andy asked for his usual Old Monk rum with soda. The old man also pointed to the chicken and fish appetizers in the menu card. The waiter wrote it all down and was just about to go, when Andy asked him for a pepperoni pizza. Mind games. He was sending a message to the old man. He wasn't taking all the shit he might have for him.

The old man smiled at him once the waiter left. He continued, 'We have learnt that Tilakpur, near Rewari, is a sleeper cell of a Pakistani terrorist organization. Three of the enemy have been staying there for the last two years. They are pretending to be Punjabi Hindus, but they aren't. We've double-checked the information. That drunkard, the Avtar chap, was killed because he had begun suspecting them.'

The wine arrived and so did Andy's Old Monk and the appetizers. Andy stared hard at the waiter. He said the pizza would be served in a minute or two. Andy sipped the rum and ignored the old man's request to sample the starters.

Andy asked, 'How can you be sure?'

'We learnt of this about a month ago. But we had to send someone inside to make sure. I know sending you without any information was a risk. But we were also sure that they wouldn't harm you. They don't want to bring the spotlight on to themselves because of petty murder.'

Andy was aghast. It was Army Intelligence who sent him into the furnace, fully aware of the challenge he was up against and not properly warning him, not even adequately equipping him with arms. That was cheap. But he stayed quiet.

'Intelligence Bureau tipped off the magazine after sharing the information with us. You might be soft on the magazinewallas, but remember, they're the ones who sent you into danger and never bothered to check back. We were the ones following your movements all the time.'

This was getting interesting for Andy. For the first time in his life, he was at the centre of it all —the terrorists, IB, the tricked magazine and the government, everyone was in on this.

It woke him up more than his drink did. He was now

on his third peg. The wine and the warmth inside had turned the old man's cheeks pink.

None of the customers at other tables were Indians. They were mostly white people from the embassies and they talked non-stop. No one bothered to look at them.

'What do you want me to do now?'

'As per the IB, the sleeper cell has become active over the last three months. They seem to be working out some kind of a plan. It could be anything... a bomb blast in Delhi, Mumbai, anywhere. Or worse, it might be a ploy to divert our attention. Like leading us on to a false trail, so that another cell, someplace else, can prepare for a terror strike without much of our attention.'

Andy nodded and the old man continued after a pause, 'Go back there. The IB will be watching your back, don't worry. Get us closer to them. They think you're a magazinewalla, no real threat. They won't kill a journalist. Just nose around, get them out in the open so that our boys can watch them.'

'What makes you think I'd be interested in this?'

'Son, I've been with Intelligence for the past forty years now. I know who is capable of what. And I also know that it was you who optioned on the last day of your Army life for service to Intelligence, if required.'

Andy remembered that day all too well. On the final day, when he reached his Commanding Officer's cabin, he was asked if he wanted to work for the country in case of national emergencies. He said yes and he was immediately asked to fill in a form and take an oath of secrecy. He had never thought much about it till last year, when they had checked his alertness and suitability.

'But that was in case of a national emergency, Sir.' This was the first time he had addressed the old man as 'Sir'.

The old man's expression was unfazed as he replied, 'We are in the middle of a national emergency, son.'

The pizza arrived with a bout of silence at the table. Andy pulled out a slice and downed it with a sip of his rum. His hunger had suddenly dissipated.

'How do I contact you?'

'Take out your phone,' the old man commanded. Andy obeyed. The old man took out his phone as well and asked Andy to look at the screen carefully.

'I have developed a system of remembering numbers by looking at the keypad. Listen carefully. The pattern of the numbers and the person being called can be related. Now look at your screen...my number is 9632147085. It starts from the last number, goes all around and finally ends with the number five, right in the middle. This signifies how I like to work, outwards to inwards.'

Andy was confused and the old man made it easy for him. 'Remember it this way. Because if you write it down and they find it on you, that will link you to me. That would mean instant death for you. As long as they don't link you to Intelligence, you stay alive. You have to save your cover at all costs...am I clear?'

The old man added, 'You look at my number on your phone, but always call me from a pay phone when no one is tailing you. Ideally, you shouldn't call me at all! I'll always be aware of your movements. That's how we work.'

'Arms?'

'You don't need any. Journalists don't carry weapons.'

They ate in silence for a few minutes. The old man seemed at ease with his food and ate without asking why Andy was only nibbling. Perhaps he knew his state of mind. When the food was over, Andy refused the old man's offer for an ice-cream.

'I have deposited two lakh rupees in your account. Don't overspend, but don't hesitate where necessary. The money comes from the Prime Minister's secret fund, one that's not audited and controlled by very few. All the best!'

The old man was gone, leaving Andy with this final surprise. He didn't like the money part, but he convinced himself that if he was working for them, he needed the money to survive. It was fair. In any case, he didn't have much money left in the bank and Monica was already urging him to quit.

The street was deserted as most of the shops had closed by now. The car was colder and Andy shivered despite the rum and the food he had eaten. He sat contemplating his next move. Too much had happened in too short a time.

The old man had said he should head to Tilakpur at first light. It wasn't an order, but the man had looked closely for his reaction. Andy was quite excited and had agreed. He drove back through empty roads. It was late and cold for people to remain outdoors.

His usual checks confirmed that the security of his house hadn't been compromised. He seemed to be in the clear for the moment. Unless, of course, he decided to poke his nose into Tilakpur again. Andy tried to sleep but couldn't. Finally, at two he switched the television on and watched a boring movie. That put him to sleep.

Later, when Andy pulled back the curtains of his bedroom, it was still dark though it was already seven in the morning. He peeped out and couldn't see anything at all. A thick fog had enveloped the outside world. It was one of those mornings when Delhiwallas celebrated by staying under their quilts till noon. He couldn't afford this luxury, but didn't want himself to be entirely deprived of all the action either. The weather and the comfort of the security of his house finally resonated with the state of his mind and Andy Karan slept like a baby in his cradle.

5

Monica was relieved that Andy was still alive. As a result, her guilt of having sent him to Tilakpur had lightened. But she still had the readership of her magazine to bother with and therefore, she still needed to pursue the story. Andy was right. Whatever was happening at Tilakpur was big. Otherwise they wouldn't have attacked him and then left him lying by the side of the highway near the Delhi–Haryana border.

While a part of her wanted to send Andy back again to investigate further, she wasn't going to take this risk again. This time, she chose Andy over her job. The criminals wouldn't spare his life the second time. To discourage Andy from going back, she had only one option left. And that was to ask him to resign. If he wasn't a journalist any more, he wouldn't have the need to go and investigate any further.

But it was frustrating to hear from Andy that he was still going back to Tilakpur. Perhaps it was just the heat of the moment and he'd calm down later, but it was scary. Monica decided to give Andy more time and asked him to stay away from the office for a few days.

The evening Andy was at Diva with the old man, Monica received a surprising call from her boss. It was very strange of him to call her directly on her cell phone. Normally, when he had anything to discuss his assistant usually conveyed his messages and he met her in his home-office at his farmhouse.

'Monica, did you send someone to Rewari?' His voice sounded anxious.

'Yes Sir, I was following up on a lead.'

'Hmmm... and where did you get this information from?'

'An unknown caller.'

'And what did he say exactly?'

'He said something big might be brewing near Rewari. He said there was a murder...'

There was a pause and Monica was certain that her answers had made her boss' breathing more laboured.

'I want that investigation dropped,' he declared, with an air of finality.

'But, our readership...' Monica trailed off. She knew she could not disagree with her boss, but her back was against the wall and the readership curve had started to drop since that very morning, just as the statistician-cum-webmaster had forecasted.

There was another pause, but when her boss spoke next, his voice was calm and composed once again. 'Don't worry about the numbers. I want more stories from urban areas, because that is where our readers are. If we do that, the numbers will go up again. OK?' Before she could even respond, he hung up.

Odd, she thought. But seconds later she was relieved.

When Andy woke up it was ten in the morning. The first thing he did was to peep out of the window. The fog had thinned. He quickly made tea and waited for the water in the geyser to heat for a shower. After tea he packed: a pair of clothes this time and all the other standard survival equipment. He missed a gun for protection, but knew that the old man was right. If discovered by his adversaries, it was a sure ticket to hell.

Showered and feeling rested, Andy drove off towards Rewari just like he did a few days ago. But by the time he reached Gurgaon he saw the futility of getting there in the daylight. He would be walking straight into their lap. And they would now surely be watching the entry points. His car was another problem. They had seen it and it could easily be identified.

He left the car at a friend's house on Sohna Road in Gurgaon and told him that he would be back after a few days to collect it. Then he walked towards the highway, ate lunch at a local restaurant, and took a bus from the bustling Rajiv Chowk to Rewari. It was a circuitous route via Sohna, but he didn't mind. The travelling time was four hours. It meant he would reach one hour after sunset. This suited his plans well. Those who might be looking for him would not expect him to arrive in a state transport bus and the darkness would hide him perfectly.

The bus was full of villagers. Men and women with transparent expressions returning from the big city, their eyes still wide open due to all the glass and cement they had seen. Many would get down at the villages on the way. He guessed there would hardly be anyone going right up to Rewari, because people from Rewari now had the money to drive their own cars to visit Delhi or Gurgaon whenever they wanted.

He bought his ticket and got a seat next to a man in a turban, who was busy puffing away in short bursts on his *bidi*. Andy thought of complaining to the man because the smoke was irritating him, but that meant giving away his pedigree. He pretended not to notice, like he was one of them. No one paid any particular attention to him either, as the bus driver tried hard to negotiate potholes on the road.

Andy's plan was to stick to his theory of being a journalist if someone asked. There were villages all around and people got in and out of the bus as it stopped after every few kilometres on their peripheries.

Four hours later when the bus crossed the turn that led to Tilakpur, Andy craned his head out of the dried vomit-spattered windows to look. The bus stop was deserted and so was the road beyond it. Fifteen minutes later, Andy dismounted from the bus with his small shoulder bag. He used the bag to camouflage himself and walked out of the small bus stand. There were many people on the road that evening. Vendors on the street shouted for the attention of those on the road, on bicycles, scooters and cars. Goats, cows and dogs wandered without purpose, too dazed by the noise and dust.

He paused near one vendor. A short man raised himself from behind the heap of roasted shelled groundnuts on a cart and looked at him through small, beady eyes. Andy bought two hundred grams worth and walked on. After half an hour he was out of the city. He turned left on the road that seemed to be going towards a village in the distance. He knew this village was about four kilometres west of Tilakpur. Andy, by now, had a plan.

He reached the village and stopped under a tree. He pulled out a bottle of water and ate the peanuts. This was his dinner. The village was dark and most of the people were asleep.

Andy walked through the fields to reach Tilakpur. It took him more than an hour and by the time he arrived, he was very tired. It was dark and cold. But the good thing was he knew his way around as he had made mental notes on his first visit. He waited at the edge of the village till midnight. He then pussyfooted into Tilakpur.

It was a dark night and the shadows made the village seem more menacing. The wind blew, making strange sounds and Andy continued walking, keeping close to the walls through narrow alleys. When he was in an alley which he thought was parallel to Ram Avtar's house, he paused and looked around a bit more carefully. One house seemed abandoned. He almost jumped with joy.

Noticing that the thorny bush near the entrance was disturbed, he decided to climb the wall. He wanted to avoid running into anyone, in case, like him, someone else also needed a place to hide. Was this really a possibility? Probably not, but he wanted to sharpen the skills he had learnt during training.

The training lesson turned out to be helpful in the end. When he dropped inside the walled house and moved closer he heard sounds. There was an urgency in them. Slowly, he moved towards the source of the sounds. He smiled when he saw a man and a woman intertwined together, the man on top of the woman. They were having sex, right there on the grass. Though he couldn't see them clearly, the sounds made it obvious to him. It felt odd to wait while they finished. But he did.

He didn't have to wait for very long. The sounds stopped with the final muffled moans of pleasure. Then he heard a few murmurs and as he watched them go, there was silence again. Now the walled house was all for him. It was a safe place indeed, or the couple, who surely were having an illegitimate relationship, wouldn't have chosen it.

Andy didn't like the smell of spent sex that he had to deal with. He was aroused and somehow, his thoughts went to Monica. It left him disgusted as he had never looked at Monica that way. She seemed happy without him getting any closer.

He climbed the roof and looked beyond carefully. By now his eyes had adjusted to the dark and he was sure of what he was doing. The entrance to Ram Avtar's house was visible, but the house was cloaked in darkness. He looked around and saw light coming from one of the houses at the end of the alley. He climbed down and walked around the other side to approach the house.

Before doing anything else, Andy wanted to see if anyone was watching the road that came in from the city. In less than fifteen minutes he was successful in spotting the man. He had nearly missed him, until a *bidi* was lit. The man was not far from where he stood, maybe about twenty feet. In the light he saw the man's features. He sat hunched and looked middle-aged. He had no business sitting like that in the middle of the night. Was he the watchmen of his handlers who sat in the lit house in the distance? A picket, in surveillance terms? It seemed likely.

Andy knew what to do. He approached the man from behind. When he was within striking distance, he took a long breath and put his hand on the man's mouth. He struggled and Andy pressed his throat with the other hand. Then he paused for a second and whispered in his ears, 'You make one sound and I'll twist your neck. You'll die in seconds. Now, I'm going to remove my hand from your mouth but you will not shout. Is it clear?'

The man nodded. Andy slowly removed his hand. The man turned towards him. Before Andy could say a word, the man shouted, 'Help, chor, chor...!'

Andy hadn't expected this reaction. He hit the man in his solar plexus with all his strength. The man gasped for breath and writhed in pain simultaneously. Andy kicked him in the same spot again, as he collapsed to the dusty ground. But the damage was already done. He couldn't afford to waste any more time. He knew the cry for help had carried all through the village that had been silent like a recuperating ghost.

Andy began running in the direction of the village he had come from. He heard sounds behind him, but it seemed like the villagers had first arrived to where Andy had left the unknown guard, trying to figure out what had happened. Once he was in darkness, he turned left twice, running towards the opposite side. He didn't stop till he saw houses against the dark sky. Sunrise was a few hours away and once the sun was out he would be noticed in no time. And if this village too had accomplices of those in Tilakpur, his fate was doomed. He continued to run to his left. A hillock rose against the sky. As he reached the base, Andy had a sudden brainwave. Hillocks in India usually have small temples at the top. It would be a perfect place to hide and rest. Maybe, if he was lucky, find some food and water too.

His hunch was right, the hill did have a temple at the top. He found whitewashed stairs leading to the small altar. Andy climbed them slowly, his senses alert. It was tiring, but he made it in the end well before the crack of dawn. The temple was a disappointment. It was a small white room, tinier than a bathroom with a roof that was barely three feet high. It was pitch dark inside and Andy knew lighting his phone-torch would give him away if anyone looked at the hill from kilometres down. He went around the small structure and found no one. Like many others in the area, this was an unattended temple with no valuables.

He sat in the distance and waited for sunrise. It was very cold and he shivered. The bag felt heavy on his shoulders and he put it down next to him.

An hour later, at the break of dawn, the world slowly

started to take shape around him. The temple was the first thing he noticed. It was really tiny. There was a bunch of bananas and a coconut kept before the small stone figurines. The bananas looked fresh and he ate a few. But he stiffened as he heard sounds. Human voices coming his way. He retracted behind the temple and lowered himself along the slope, hiding behind a bush.

Andy heaved a sigh of relief. They were just local devotees, around five villagers in all. They had milk and other offerings in their hands. They lit incense sticks, stuck them into old, rock hard potatoes, folded their hands and stood in a prayer. Though they only murmured, Andy had an idea of what they wanted. They needed rain for their crops and peace and tranquillity in their village. He couldn't guarantee the rains, but he could surely try bringing them some peace. He would find out what was happening there. He felt powerful and strong.

Andy had never prayed in his life. Yet every time he saw people spending time and money to seek blessings from someone who did not exist, he was moved by the enormity of their faith. Perhaps they were blessed, to believe in the invisible. When they were gone, Andy came out of his hideout and drank the milk they had left in earthen cups. It was fresh and sweet and he felt blessed.

Soon more voices came his way and he scrambled back to his hiding spot. This time someone caught his attention. It was Ram Avtar's wife. He was sure it was her.

When this group left, Andy followed them down the stairs, making sure he kept slightly out of sight. The fog was just beginning to settle, making it somewhat easy for him. The villagers were walking without a worry in the world. They had left all their worries in the good care of God moments ago, they had nothing to fear any more. No one turned even once. When the crowd dispersed at the bottom, Andy found Ram Avtar's wife breaking away from the group and continuing her journey alone. He followed after her and when they were in the middle of a mustard field, he appeared in front of her and smiled. He hoped she wouldn't scream and she didn't.

'I know you. You came to my house the other day. What are you doing here?'

Andy explained that all he wanted was to ask her a few questions. An act, for which he was mercilessly beaten and thrown on the Delhi border, left to die. But he was lucky as someone called for help. He said he had spent three days in the hospital for no mistake of his. All facts. He didn't want to lie to her.

She looked concerned and said, 'I don't understand why so many people want to know about my husband. When he was alive, he was a drunkard and no one ever bothered to correct him. Everyone made fun of me instead.' She lost her composure and sat in the field, as tears forced their way from her large dark eyes.

Andy didn't know what to say. 'I think your life might

be in danger.'

He had to say this sooner or later, because he really believed that her life was in danger. She looked up and said, 'I'm not bothered about my life. I worry for my daughter. She is just eighteen and they have their eyes on her.'

'Who are they?'

'The same people who killed my husband.'

'Do you know who they are?' Andy persisted.

'I'm not sure, but there are some strange people who have been staying in our village for the past two years or so. They sleep all day and play cards at night. They're big and scary and speak in a funny accent. I think they are Punjabis.'

'What do they do in the village?'

'I have no idea. They don't seem to do anything and yet they spend a lot of money.'

'What's your name?'

'Gulabo.'

'Nice name,' Andy said without meaning it. She said nothing. He was wondering how much he could tell her and how much he could trust her. In a minute he was able to organize his thoughts and he slowly explained, 'They are bad people. They killed your husband and now they are eyeing your daughter. They might kill her too. They tried to kill me already. This explains that they are on opposite sides of me, you and your daughter.'

She nodded. She appeared to be a courageous woman.

'If we are together in this, we will be able to nail them. But to do that we first need proof of what they're up to here. Can you try and be more watchful...keep an eye on anything unusual? I'll meet you at the temple tomorrow morning. Do you come here every day?'

She nodded. Andy smiled. They talked for a few more minutes and then she walked towards Tilakpur.

6

A ndy had switched his cell phone off in Delhi. He knew his enemies could easily track his movements using it. They seemed to be well-equipped and established. He wanted to speak to Monica, coax her for additional information. Currently, all he had was Gulabo. He couldn't risk going into Tilakpur as people would be watching it from all sides. By now they must have figured out that he came in from the rear.

He returned to the temple and wondered what he would do next. Going to Rewari seemed a good idea, as the enemy must have called their men back to Tilakpur to re-access the situation. They'd increase vigil, no doubt. Probably they had nothing at Rewari.

His bag was becoming a problem. It was heavy and his shoulders ached. He pulled out a strong polythene bag he carried for this exact reason and got rid of the bag along the slope of the hillock, at the base of a shrub. He paused to make sure from a distance of about six feet and he couldn't see a thing. The bag was safe for the time being.

Andy left at midday, keeping to the fields, his head almost level with the majestic mustard crop that grew in abundance in the state. It was easy now without the bag and he could walk about four kilometres in an hour. Two hours later, he was at Rewari.

He headed straight to the barman, Rohtas' house. Even if a few villains still remained at Rewari, in a crowded city and in broad daylight he had nothing to fear. They wouldn't plan an attack in the open and risk the attention of the local police. He sensed their helplessness and smiled.

Rohtas' house was small — a door facing a narrow lane with two rooms inside it. An old lady answered his knock and said he wasn't in. She had no idea where he was for the last two days. She said she didn't remember his number and closed the door. Her answers were too predictable, too rehearsed. Someone surely had tutored her to reply in this manner. He wanted to find out if his hunch was correct.

Andy knocked again. The old woman came to the door once again and looked at him patiently. Another hint. Old women are never patient with an unwanted guest who wasn't keen to go away from their door.

'I have come from Gurgaon. I'm here to offer my cousin's hand in marriage. I've been referred by Shashi Kant Sharma.'

The old lady was foxed. She didn't know what to say. Whoever tutored her never thought of this one.

Andy leaned forward and whispered, 'I know he's inside. Tell him I'm here to save his life from these thugs... just tell him that.'

She turned and walked in, leaving the door open. Seconds later, a man appeared and asked him to step inside. Andy hesitated and the man smiled. He said his name was Rohtas and that he worked as a barman at the Blue Soda bar.

Andy walked into the house, making sure that he left the door open.

They sat in plastic chairs. There was no furniture in the room, except the chairs. The walls were bare too. The delicious aroma of simple, cooked food floated around them. The man's clothes were old and worn out. There was no doubt that he was poor. The question was, was he ambitious? Poor, ambitious people can be very dangerous. They can go to any extent to achieve their goals, especially to earn money and become rich. What mattered to them was the end, not the means. Andy wanted to be sure of that.

'My name is Andy. I understand you were friends with

Ram Avtar.'

'Yes, I was his friend. But he died a year ago.' The man was calmer than a barman should be and he didn't ask the reason for these questions.

'Who killed him?'

'I have no idea. He was a regular at the bar. He was nice, but perhaps he drank more than required. He was addicted to alcohol!'

'But that doesn't mean someone should kill him.'

'He had a habit of picking arguments in the bar, and even outside it. I guess he must have said something insulting to someone and was consequently killed by him in a fit of rage. He was killed on the way from the bar to his house.'

The man was not revealing much.

'I want to know who all he met...Do you think he had enemies? Do you think some of your customers might not be residents of Rewari or nearby villages?'

'We don't keep a record of who comes and goes. And I'm not sure if he had enemies. Look, I liked the man. He was a simpleton. I told him several times to control his drinking and take care of his family... but he wouldn't listen.'

'All right, I want you to keep a check on your customers from here on. If you see anyone who is not from this region and is also not a tourist, please observe the person carefully and tell me when I meet you next.'

'But who are you?'

'I'm from the Delhi Police.'

'No, you're not...Delhi Police doesn't behave this way. You look more like a *fauji* to me...'

Andy didn't like this. He wanted to keep his hair long, but old habits die hard. With his crew cut and his mannerisms, any Tom, Dick and Harry could figure out that he was a *fauji*.

'No, I'm not a *fauji*. I'm a journalist.'

Andy shook hands with Rohtas and left shortly afterwards. He had no idea why Rohtas wasn't alarmed at seeing him and asking those questions. He seemed like someone who was in control, someone who was in charge. But what was he in charge of?

He decided to monitor Rohtas' movements as there was no point in returning to the temple and he couldn't go into Tilakpur either. There was a *dhaba* at the end of the lane. He sat there and hid behind a newspaper, pretending to read. Four cups of tea and a big lunch later, he finally saw the barman emerge from his house. He was on a motorcycle. Andy dropped some money on the table and quickly hailed an autorickshaw. He followed the man. When he didn't stop at the Blue Soda bar and drove out of the city, he was worried where the man was headed. The autorickshaw driver said he couldn't go very far. On the outskirts of Rewari, when they were well past the road that led to Tilakpur and the barman continued to drive, Andy had an idea where he was headed. It had to be Delhi, perhaps to inform his bosses about his strange visitor. He might have even taken his picture while he sat in the house. Rohtas did ask him to sit at a particular spot, saying it was warmer there.

The autorickshaw driver had started protesting more vehemently now. He finally stopped and Andy got down cursing his luck. Fortunately, a bus came up right behind him, with the Delhi–Rewari label on it. He waved frantically and thankfully, the driver jerked to a stop. He hopped in, bought a ticket for Delhi and sat down in the front seat. The bus was almost empty.

He could see the man right in front of the bus. In a moment he realized the futility of the whole exercise. You can't chase a motorcycle on a bus. Yet, he continued to sit. An hour later, on the outskirts of Gurgaon, the motorcycle stopped while the bus continued further towards Delhi. A hundred metres ahead, he walked up to the driver and asked him to stop. Thankfully, he obliged and Andy hopped off a slowing bus. He turned around, but the motorcycle was no longer on the road. He walked to the spot where it had stopped and looked around.

There was a restaurant on the side of the road. Several cars were parked outside. As were a few motorcycles. Andy walked to the parking lot and realised that the restaurant did not have a clear view of the road. He shuffled around the entrance and spotted the barman in no time. He was seated at the end with a grey-haired man, both their backs towards Andy. The two of them were engaged in a conversation. Half the tables were occupied.

Andy walked out. There was a curio shop outside for the tourists, and he bought a golf cap from there. It added to his confidence and now he could get closer and take a seat nearer to their table. He asked for tea and strained his ears to hear. But he couldn't. Minutes ticked by and he asked for another cup of tea. People came in and went out. The smell of fennel seeds hung in the air as all the tables had one big bowl and customers stuffed mouthfuls of it before leaving.

An hour later, Rohtas and the man with grey hair got up together and walked out. They crossed his table. He tilted his head an inch more, but they seemed oblivious of his presence. Seconds later, Andy walked to the entrance and peeped out. Rohtas was now seeing off the man, who had come in a car. As the man slid into the driver's seat, Andy got a better look at him. It was the old man he had met at Diva at Greater Kailash II! Andy's heart skipped a beat.

This case had the government's backing, the old man had said. So why was he meeting a barman whom Andy was entrusted to meet? Rohtas and the old man also seemed to be on an equal footing. Was he being fooled into believing that he was working for the Government of India? Was he the scapegoat being taken for a walk before his head was chopped off? Things didn't quite add up. Perhaps Monica knew about this and therefore, wanted him to keep out of this case. Andy looked on, dumbstruck.

The barman got into the car after the old man. Perhaps they were going somewhere to meet others.

There was a tap on his back. He slowly turned and found himself looking into a waiter's eyes. The waiter was smiling, as if he was an old acquaintance.

'What?' Andy was annoyed and it showed.

'Sa'ab, the old man in the car is calling you.'

'Who?' Andy asked and turned to figure it out for himself. He saw the old man looking straight at him and smiling. He was also waving, signalling for him to come over.

Andy didn't realize how slowly he was walking. His mind was at work. Has he already been framed? He was sure they had not seen him, so how did they come to know he was there? Was the waiter involved too? Did this hotel and all the others along the highway have his photographs circulated by the old man?

He stood still once at the car. The old man was standing near the car door and the barman was right next to him. Andy was ushered into the back seat. He hesitated and the old man said, 'Don't worry!' He got in.

The old man climbed in after him, while the barman sat in the passenger seat in front. This meant they were not going anywhere. A good sign.

'OK, it's time for introductions. Andy, this is our Inspector from the IB...he has been working undercover as a barman for the last three years. Meet Junior Intelligence Officer Dewanchand of the IB.'

Andy extended his hand, his mouth open with surprise.

The old man continued, 'And this here is Captain Andy Karan.'

Andy was surprised that the old man had preferred to address him with his rank, rather than just by his name. It brought some comfort. He also didn't add the 'retired' part of it, which meant he still considered him active in service. Another good sign. Andy smiled and said hello to the barman.

In a new voice, the barman responded with a happy smile. Though he was still wearing the same worn clothes from the morning, his demeanour had changed by now. His eyes were sharp and his face composed.

'We don't have much time, but remember Andy, you must visit and share information with him only when really required. He has better access to me, so if you have something for me, pass it to him. It'll be easier. By the way, you can call me Mr. Kapoor.'

Andy briefed them about the progress he had made so far. He said he was still to meet Ram Avtar's police constable friend, but he had befriended the dead man's wife and she had agreed to help. He would have more information very soon.

After the old man drove off towards Delhi and the barman left the other way, Andy walked back inside the restaurant and asked for another cup of tea. He wanted to clear his head as the events of the last hour had completely derailed some of the theories that had started to form in his mind.

Monica had been trying to call Andy all day. But his phone was switched off. She was worried about him. Technically, since he had not sent his resignation yet, he was still working for the magazine. What if he hadn't cooled off and had gone back to Tilakpur? She shuddered at the thought.

Her boss was very clear. The investigation was to be dropped. She had no idea why he wanted to drop it, but she was not interested. In any case, if there was an intelligence situation brewing, it was not the magazine's problem. She didn't have to worry about the subscribers' numbers any more. It was such a huge relief that she didn't want to question her boss's decision. She was merely an employee and if a decision suited her, she wasn't prepared to give it much thought.

But Andy was different and that was the root cause of her crisis. Inability to trace Andy was raising her anxiety. She even thought of going to Tilakpur herself, just to check out her theory. But considering the risk of her boss discovering this and the troubles at Tilakpur, she quickly ruled out this option.

An idea struck her at that moment. She knew Andy's cell phone number and with a cell phone number, a lot could be found out these days. Just like the IP address of an internet connection. She called up her friend in a communications company and asked for the information. Her friend got back to her an hour later. Her answer eased Monica's nerves. She was told that the phone was last used at Noida and since then it had been switched off.

Andy probably needed some more time to think things through, she thought, and got back to her work. Monica decided to call him again after two days.

7

From the restaurant on National Highway 8, Andy took a bus back to Rewari. The old, battered white and blue Haryana Roadways buses were turning into his favourite transport service of late. The window next to his seat in the bus couldn't be closed properly and cold air came gushing in as the bus sped along the truck-laden highway. He slid away from it and looked around. Empty faces of the kind he had travelled with earlier, stared out of the bus with vacant eyes. He was surprised to see how little people spoke to each other.

Andy didn't know what to expect from this case any more. He didn't know who was on whose side here. Even his own boss, a person he considered a friend, wouldn't tell him what to expect before sending him off into the snake pit. And after tonight, he didn't know what to make of this Kapoor fellow either. Whose side was he really on?

Andy needed to be sure whose hands he was gift-wrapping his life into.

Andy fished out his cell phone. He sat staring at the phone for a long time on the rickety bus ride, and finally switched it on. There was only one man likely to give him any help at this time of the night. And, it was someone he could trust. Andy dialled a number and waited for the line to connect. A thick, gruff voice barked at the other end.

'Brigadier Joshi!'

Brigadier Joshi had been Andy's Commanding Officer during his last posting in Drass, Kashmir. It was he who pushed Andy a sheaf of papers on his last day in the force. He knew Andy well, he knew he'd make a fine soldier in Intelligence. And now, Andy needed his help to set his head straight.

'Sir, this is Captain Andy Karan... I served under you in Drass.'

'Andy! Good to hear from you, my boy! How's life beyond the fatigues? What have you been up to these days?'

Andy rattled off everything that happened over the last three years, his foray into investigative journalism and then spoke in extensive detail about his current assignment, making sure to reveal only the broader picture. He told Joshi about Kapoor and asked, 'Sir, I need a favour from you. The way this thing is going, I'm really lost here. I don't know who's playing whom here. I need to know more about this Kapoor chap, I need to know if he really is who he's saying he is...'

Joshi was alert all through Andy's monologue. He had kept making his trademark grunts, more to confirm that he was still listening. He now replied, 'Son, give me a couple of hours and I'll see what I can do.'

Andy thanked his former CO and hung up, switching off his phone along with it too. He had told Joshi that he'd call him back, and Joshi knew why. All he could do now was wait for the hours to pass, and pray that Joshi would be able to get back with some real information.

The bus arrived in darkness and Andy dismounted about a hundred metres short of the bus stand as it slowed to negotiate a turn. Getting down at the bus stand now had greater risk as he had attacked their man at Tilakpur. They must have discovered that he had not arrived by car this time. The only two other ways of getting in to Rewari from Delhi were either by bus, or by train. In addition to watching all the sides of the village, they were surely watching the buses and trains arriving.

It was dark and he took the inner lanes to reach the other end of the city. There was an inconspicuous *dhaba* under a newly constructed road bridge and Andy decided to eat there before leaving for the temple. He asked for egg *bhurji* and buttered *tandoori roti*.

It was very cold and he had a running nose because of the bus journey. He wanted alcohol to enliven his mood and fight the cold, but there were no shops around. When he asked, he realized the *dhaba* didn't serve liquor either. He ate casually as he noticed the world around him. Trucks were parked near the *dhaba* and the drivers were busy eating their food, seated on airy cots. Some smoked in-house *hookahs*, which seemed to be complimentary. The rest of the evening was eventless. His phone remained switched off and nobody paid any special attention to him.

Andy pulled a newspaper lying on the next table and started leafing through it, more to waste time than anything else. Finally, he walked up to the STD booth next to the *dhaba* and called Joshi. The brigadier picked up the phone on the first ring.

'Andy! Tough luck, son... this thing isn't going any further!'

At first, Andy's shoulders drooped. Another dead end. 'I don't understand, Sir... what's not going any further?'

'I've been trying to access the IB database, but every time I search for Kapoor, it says I need higher clearance to get through. Now either he really is someone high up in the hierarchy, or else he's been pissing them off really badly. I'm sorry, son, this bugger could swing either way!'

There was nothing more for Andy to do there. He

thanked Brigadier Joshi for all his help and hung up once again.

After finishing with a Hindi newspaper that he was still reading, Andy realized he still had to meet the policeman, Ram Avtar's other friend. He hired an auto rickshaw, crossed the bus stand and reached the opposite side of the city.

Andy lazily watched the road snake away from him towards Delhi. The police personnel's accommodation was to his left. An imposing wrought iron gate kept the houses well-guarded. He wondered if there was a need for the police to make a large barricade around the area they themselves lived in. Somehow, it didn't send the right signals — as in, if the police didn't consider their own families safe, who else could.

Since there was no police station sanctioned for Tilakpur, a police outpost on the edge of Rewari gave it jurisdictional cover. He knew the constable's name he wanted to meet. Gulabo had also said he was the only one who had cried at her husband's funeral, but had never visited since then.

Andy wondered if he should take the barman, Dewanchand's help for this. But then he decided to proceed on his own. It could be challenging, he thought, as he walked across to the gate. A small patrol booth stood on one side of the gate and through a small window in it, an oldish man smiled at him. Andy was just about to smile back at him, but refrained at the very last minute. One of the advantages of looking a *fauji* was that sometimes people also mistook them for policemen. And neither *faujis* nor policemen smiled unnecessarily. So he held on and gestured the man out.

'Sa'ab?' The man was short, about sixty and his hands shook by his sides.

'I'm here to meet Constable Ramesh Kumar. Open the gates.'

The man hesitated and looked beyond him. Andy knew the man was searching for the vehicle he had come in. People who spoke with such authority never 'walked' to their destinations.

'It's OK, my driver dropped me here and has gone to fill petrol.'

The man seemed satisfied with the excuse.

'I haven't seen Constable Ramesh Kumar for the last two days. I'm not sure if he is in. Let me check on the intercom. Who should I say is calling, sa'ab?'

'My name is Anand Singh and I know someone he knows well. Once he's on the line, I would like to speak to him.'

The man nodded in understanding and walked back to the small booth. He returned after a few minutes with the news, 'He isn't picking up the phone. As I said, I haven't seen him for the last two, maybe three days. He's not at home.'

'All right, but are you sure you dialled the right house?'

'Sa'ab, he lives in building 7, Flat D. I know it very well.'

Andy walked away after thanking him. Once he had cleared the area and was sure the old gatekeeper couldn't see him even if he wanted to, Andy stepped into the adjoining field. He penetrated through the mustard plants till he was sure no one could see him, and walked towards the police quarters in the distance. He now knew which house Constable Ramesh lived in.

The walls were high, about eight feet and he could see shards of glass on the top glinting due to the lights from the road. Andy was on the opposite side of the gate and he walked around till he found a foothold in the wall. Climbing the wall was tough. Even for a person like him who had been very good at rope climbing in the Academy during his training days. On this wall, there were far too many glass pieces. The policemen, he thought sarcastically, took their threats seriously. He was unable to scale the wall properly and nearly fell twice. When he nicked his palm and the blood came oozing out, Andy wondered if he was doing the right thing.

He climbed down, took a few long breaths, and

controlled the blood by tying his handkerchief tightly around the cut. Then he waited for the blood flow to stop. Fifteen minutes later, he was finally successful in climbing the wall and jumped inside, landing on soft ground. The block was easy to find as there was no one on the road that ran alongside it. Flat D was on the first floor. Andy took the stairs and knocked lightly at the door. After a few minutes he repeated his action. This was surprising. The door wasn't locked, but no one came from inside to open it either. Nobody had answered the gatekeeper's call on the intercom too.

Andy pushed the door gently and it swung open with a loud groan. The house was in darkness. Andy's heart was beating wildly. He felt naked without a revolver, as he moved in cautiously. He found the kitchen and searched in the darkness, till he discovered something that felt sharp on the fingers. It was a knife and holding it tightly in his hands, Andy felt somewhat better, he felt more secure.

His ears strained for any sound. There was none. Andy hugged the wall and inched forward very slowly, going further into the house. Still no sound, absolutely nothing. The bedroom door was closed. Andy crept forward, tightening his grasp around the handle of the knife and very gently pushed the door ajar. And, it hit him. A very faint, rotten odour — like the inside of a dead fridge. Andy could feel the sweat form on his forehead, as a drop trickled down and collected at the corner of his left eye. He wiped his forehead and blinked animatedly.

He began following the foul smell, slowly moving past the bed. And his worst fears were realized.

He sat on the floor and very carefully used his cell phone torch to check. A man was lying on the floor in a pool of dried blood, a gaping bullet hole at the centre of his head. His dead eyes looked at him and Andy withdrew. He stood there with bated breath. Andy realized that there was no time to lose. He began using the light from his mobile phone to check if there was anything that could provide him with some leads, maybe help him narrow down on the attacker.

He found Ramesh's pistol kept on the bedside table. Andy picked it up. It felt heavy and cold. He pulled out the magazine and found it full. When a person is murdered, his protection is usually stolen. Since this was a standard operating procedure, the police would never doubt that someone came later just to steal a pistol. Proceeding with this obvious conclusion, Andy pushed it deep into his pants, careful that the safety catch on the pistol was switched on.

Andy now turned his attention to his finger prints. He removed his handkerchief and grossly wiped the parts he thought he had touched. Not that the police had any records of his finger prints, but he just didn't want to take any chances. He hoped to stay away from the routine police trouble. And even as he started wiping out any trace of his presence in the room, Andy's mind tried to solve the ostensibly impossible riddle: Who could have killed the constable...and why?

Their enemies at Tilakpur wouldn't dare enter a police accommodation to kill a policeman. The same reason why they had left him alive — they didn't want the police to start getting involved. Whatever they were doing, they didn't want too many noses sticking near their houses. In which case, who could it be?

Andy heard the sound of feet climbing and quickly used the stairs to reach a floor up. He waited at the landing above. The feet didn't stop and continued to climb. Andy rushed up to the roof and heard them, a man and a lady, open a lock and step inside their house. With people right beneath his feet, he knew he had to walk with caution.

He had to pass this information on to the old man as soon as possible, but realized there was no point as he had no idea about the motive of the killers. The old man would anyway learn about it in a day or two as the smell reached outside and the man's death became public knowledge in the local newspaper. Andy looked in the darkness beyond, contemplating his next move. He was tired and sleepy, more so since he felt helpless and lost.

It was nearly midnight and he came down carefully and climbed the wall the same way to get out of the police residential area. By two at night, when he reached the temple on the hillock, he was so tired that he slept in the shrubs within moments of lying down.

Gulabo waited near the temple after her prayers. She had information which she was eager to pass to Andy. But it worried her no end as she couldn't see him. The previous night it became clear that Andy was right. Her hunch was proved correct too. They spoke in a language that she couldn't understand. Punjabi, surely. It was different, not what people spoke around these parts of town. Two words were repeated as the men spoke: South Block and Rashtrapati Bhawan. They also mentioned the police and Murud Janjira a number of times. As they talked in the courtyard below, she had heard them from the terrace of the adjoining house, peeping into the darkness of the night.

Gulabo had been worried sick about her daughter. So, earlier in the morning, she had sent her with her cousin brother to her mother's house about fifty kilometres away. Only after her mother called to confirm that she had reached home safely, Gulabo decided on her future course of action. In the days before her husband's death, there were times when she thought he wanted to say something. But her state of mind was such that she never paid any attention to him. Her husband had failed her completely. He disrespected her, didn't earn enough and physically tortured their daughter. He hadn't always been like that and she had seen better days. But once he became addicted to alcohol, he was beyond control.

The day Andy told her that he was attacked and beaten up so badly that he could have died, she had decided to help him. He looked like a sensible young man to her. If she had a son, perhaps he would have been like him. She felt sympathetic towards him, because he was beaten mercilessly for no reason. She had also never thought of the danger these unknown men could bring on other innocent people, till Andy told her. Somehow it seemed to be the honourable thing for her to do. She had no fear.

Now she waited for Andy. Her daily companions had finished their prayers and were slowly moving towards the stairs. One of them called her name over her shoulder. Uncertain, she joined them. Once at the base of the hillock, when people went their different ways, she walked to the spot she had met Andy and waited, hands on her hips, looking around her. She waited for half an hour and slowly walked back to her house in Tilakpur. She felt even more confused now.

Gulabo reached her house, opened the lock and walked in. She was thirsty and filled a glass from the earthen pitcher kept in a *jharokha* in the courtyard. She sat down on the charpoy, her mind still on Andy, and absent-mindedly sipped her water. She finished drinking, but the glass fell from her hand. She looked up at the sky and it began to spin. Then without any control over herself, she slipped into unconsciousness.

Andy woke up with a start. The sun was out, but it was

still early morning. He looked at his watch. It was seven. Perhaps he had missed Gulabo by a few minutes. It made him angry, but he knew he had to control his emotions to survive this mess. He peeped from his hiding spot and realized there was no one in front of the temple. He walked up and removed the milk and fruits and ate in a hurry. The devotees had all come and gone. That meant Gulabo had left too. What if she had some information for him? He kicked himself. He didn't like the prospect of waiting till tomorrow morning to meet Gulabo. He decided to go to Tilakpur. If he took the necessary precautions they wouldn't be able to see him. And now he had a gun too.

Andy climbed down and walked through the fields to reach outside the village. He stopped about hundred metres from the periphery. From there, he took about fifteen minutes to monitor for any unusual movements. He picked each house and looked at it closely for a minute or so, before moving to the next one. He saw a few people walking, dogs sniffing about and buffaloes being taken to the pond, but nothing looked overtly suspicious. He had earlier changed into fresh white trousers, a white shirt and a jacket.

Cautiously he walked in, the pistol rubbing against the small of his back with each step, as if repeating its assurance. He had used the entry point that was the farthest from the house he had earlier seen lit during the night, the house he thought the suspects lived in. People crossed him and he watched them. The boy with his two teeth missing was walking a buffalo home today and waved his stick at him gleefully. Andy smiled.

He reached Gulabo's house, paused to see left and right and knocked on the door. It was opened by a man he didn't recognize. The man smiled and waved him to an empty charpoy in the courtyard. Andy hesitated, but walked inside and sat on it, not sure if he was doing the right thing. Three people, as if in answer, appeared from a room and stood facing him, their big arms crossed against their chests. Andy instinctively reached for his pistol, but they were faster. They pounced on him. While two of them pressed his face against the rope mesh in the charpoy, the third recovered his pistol. Then one of them tied his hands at his back. They returned to their positions, the hands once again against their chests. It was too theatrical, as if someone was staging a performance in front of him.

Andy waited. These men looked tough and their eyes were remote. Probably they were going to kill him. He kicked himself for the disaster. He had stupidly walked into their trap. They had captured him again. Everyone had warned him — the old man, the IB inspector, and even Monica. But he had been stupid. For the first time, he thought about the uselessness of his fight. Why was he fighting? Who was he protecting? He wasn't working with the intelligence full-time or the police, or the IB, and yet he had risked his life — not once, but twice. Was he the only person who could have done this job? The old man Kapoor said they knew this village had a sleeper cell. Then why had nobody done anything about it? He, an Ex-Army officer, who was working as a journalist was used as bait. How stupid of him to have accepted this. It was surely the result of watching too many Hollywood movies.

He thought of telling them that he was merely a journalist, maybe beg for mercy. But they wouldn't believe him now, particularly after they had recovered his pistol. A state police pistol with a full magazine. Another of his stupid misadventures. For the first time in his life, Andy understood the feelings of a trapped rabbit.

How right his mother was to name him Karan, he thought ruefully. His impractical generosity in accepting this job had brought his end.

8

Intelligence officer Dewanchand loved his job with the Intelligence Bureau (IB). There was no office, no routine, no strict timings and a faraway boss. As an undercover agent he could do anything that he loved doing and still be paid for his designation in full.

As a barman at the Blue Soda bar he had a comfortable life. He would arrive at five each evening, prepare the bar for the night and return home at one in the morning. He had a tacit understanding with the owner, who paid him a thousand rupees less than the other three bar waiters for not washing the utensils at the end of the day. Dewanchand had convinced him that he had inherited a large family property and he needed to work only to occupy himself. An empty mind is a devil's workshop was his favourite idiom, and as it turned out, the bar owner's too. They clicked well together.

As a barman he had access to the people and he didn't have to do the dirty work either. It suited him well. He would eavesdrop wherever and whenever he wanted, without people taking him seriously. And people talked in bars. They talked about themselves, about others, about what they feared. They talked about money, how to make it, how best to spend it. They discussed luxuries that only money could buy and dreamt of making it big. After three drinks everyone in the bar behaved like they were successful businessmen and spoke in broken English. Without knowing Dewanchand's background, they insisted during late hours, that he spoke to them in English too, and sometimes made half-hearted attempts in teaching him a few sentences. He would speak the words incorrectly and they would wave him away, laughing at him.

Dewanchand was the reason why Andy was at Tilakpur. Through careful hearing over a long period of time, he had learnt about the existence of a possible sleeper cell at Tilakpur. Such findings are not concluded in a day. It takes months, sometimes years, to put the scraps of information together, analyse them, corroborate with other intelligence operatives before concluding with reasonable certainty. Once he was sure, he had passed the findings on to his boss. But after a few weeks, his boss at Chandigarh issued him revised orders, directing him to report to a certain Mr Kapoor at New Delhi.

After that he started passing information to Mr Kapoor regularly through channels that were established for the purpose. Each week he would go to Gaffar Market in Karol Bagh and meet an old man at a tea shop and pass him a bunch of notebook papers, comprising all that he had learnt over the days. The situation worsened over a period of time and one day he heard someone whisper that raw material had arrived for the attacks. He had called Mr Kapoor that day from an STD booth.

Dewanchand had been worried about Andy. He thought Andy was too raw to be used for such an important operation. He also didn't like the fact that Mr Kapoor and the Government of India used him as an expendable. The young man was unduly taking too many risks, something which no one else was prepared to take. But he also knew how intelligence worked. So instead of getting worried, he had decided to wait and watch. In any case, sending a journalist inside Tilakpur was a better idea than a regular intelligence operative.

The afternoon Andy walked into the trap at Tilakpur, Dewanchand decided to visit the village. It was something he wasn't expected to do, but as a friend of the dead Ram Avtar he thought he could use the opportunity. He drove his bike into the village and walked to Ram Avtar's house on foot from the edge of the lane. The door was closed, but not locked from outside. So he knocked and waited. Silence. He knocked again. No one came to open the door. He tried to push his weight on to the door, but he realized that the door was bolted from inside.

Dewanchand could smell trouble from experience. He realized the vulnerability of the situation. It was not possible to tackle the problem alone, so he walked across to the neighbouring house and asked them if they knew why Gulabo, Ram Avtar's widow, was not opening the door. The concerned neighbours, a man and his two young sons, joined him. They pushed the door a few times and finally, it gave way. On a charpoy in the courtyard sat a dazed Andy, his hands tied behind, his mouth taped. Next to him, on the ground, was Gulabo, her eyes half open.

There was no one else in sight. While the others rushed to Gulabo, Dewanchand untied Andy's hands.

'Second time lucky! How many were there?' he winked at Andy, trying to comfort him.

'Thanks for saving my life...three of them, never seen them before.'

Gulabo told them what she had heard. She sounded weak, but managed to cover all the details. Dewanchand asked the neighbours to call for medical help. He felt her forehead and pulse. She seemed to be recovering. From her narration of events, he understood that she was sedated. Someone had laced her drinking water with drugs. The same people trapped Andy. But why didn't they kill them? Perhaps he got there in time. Andy had already thanked him for saving his life. But where were the attackers?

They visited the suspected house, but it was empty — both of people and their belongings. There was nothing of interest there. It was clear that whoever lived in the house had left it for good. It seemed well planned, not in a hurry, as nothing lay scattered.

'Looks like Tilakpur will soon turn into a nondescript village again.' Andy shook hands with Dewanchand, thanked Gulabo and walked out of the house. The first thing he did was to visit the temple on the hillock to collect his bag.

He walked back to the main highway. He was at peace now. He knew they could have killed him, but were ordered not to. While he and Gulabo waited for their fate, the men kept checking their phone for messages. Before a decision could be ordered, Dewanchand arrived and they left jumping off the back wall as the door was being pushed open by the barman and the villagers.

One thing was clear. These were people who obeyed orders. There was someone running the show from faraway. But the question was from where? Pakistan, or Nepal, or could it even be Bangladesh? When Andy reached the highway, he took a bus and got off at Rajiv Chowk two hours later. He walked to his friend's house and thanked his wife for watching over his car. His friend was still at office and he declined her offer for food, though he was famished. He just didn't have the energy to engage in small talk any more. He had survived a certain near-death situation less than two hours ago. Driving his car back towards Delhi, Andy tried to come to terms with that fact.

This wasn't the first time he had seen death from

such close quarters. He could recall at least two occasions where he had to undertake almost suicidal missions in the terrorist-infested Kupwara district of Kashmir. But he was just a shade over twenty then, and his sense of life was different from what it was now. The incident this afternoon, he thought, was not a worthy way to have died. Death by unknown people, without even getting a fair chance to fight. And this time he wasn't even on a proper job, he was just there for the heck of it.

Andy turned his phone on again and called Monica. She answered on the first ring and he smiled as he said he was in Delhi and that everything was OK. She asked him to come to the office immediately. Andy agreed and said he was on his way. An hour later, he was standing outside her cabin door. She had been worried about him, it was written all over her face. But she was still his boss; he kept reminding himself.

Monica saw him standing outside through her office glass panels. She rushed up to the door and smiled. Asking him to come in, she shut the door sharply and immediately snapped the venetian blinds on the panels shut. Then, without another word, she spun around on her heels and hugged him. It was somewhat awkward, but it felt nice. For once, Andy stopped reminding himself that she was his boss. She was just Monica in that split second.

As they sat down, Andy agreed for a coffee but turned down her offer for a cigarette.

'So, what's new?' Monica asked, lighting a slim cigarette. She thought of telling him about her boss asking her to drop the investigation at Tilakpur, but then decided against it. She didn't want to rekindle Andy's interest in Tilakpur once again.

'Nothing.' The cigarette looked good between her shapely fingers, he thought. 'You asked me to quit the job, so I've been thinking about my options.' Andy didn't know what else to say.

'Don't quit. Stay. I was worried about you that day. I thought I would lose someone dear to me.' Her voice trailed off. Another of that awkward moment.

They didn't say anything for a minute, waiting for the other to speak. Then both started off together and laughed. It was like in a movie and Andy wondered if it was possible to fall in love with her. He immediately admonished himself silently for thinking like this about his boss. About Monica.

They drank their coffees in silence after they ran out of words. But not before they had spoken briefly about their lives, what they liked, or disliked, their goals, ambitions, put-offs. Andy thought he understood her better now. Monica had had a tough life. She fell in love twice, but was abandoned by both her lovers. She had sounded distant when she said this. Andy wanted to imagine her pain. But couldn't. He kept a wooden face and wondered what kind of a moron would abandon a woman like

Monica. But perhaps he didn't know her that well either. Maybe she was dominating, or eccentric, or demanding. People behave differently in relationships as compared to their jobs.

Andy watched her closely. She was looking out of the window. The late afternoon sunlight fell on her face. Her eyes seemed to be gazing at the mid-distance nothing. He saw the right mix of mystery and charm in them. Yet there were shades of pain, which he had spotted earlier but didn't know the reason for. Here was a beautiful woman who just wanted love from life. She was desirable, educated and employed. Yet lonely.

Andy's eyes slipped down to her breasts. The sunlight had made her cotton dress somewhat translucent and he didn't have to imagine anything that he wished to see. He felt guilty, but was also aroused at the same time. Monica didn't move, her eyes still looking outside. Andy's brain slowed down as his arousal began to take greater control of his senses. Monica moved her lips slightly and his eyes jumped on them. They looked like pink candies waiting to be licked. She parted them slightly and he could see her tongue licking her teeth.

'So, what are you going to do now?' Monica suddenly turned and Andy almost fell out of his chair. He knew he looked horrible and quickly brought his feelings under check.

'Nothing... I think I'll make a move now.' He quickly

got up, collected his car keys from the table.

Monica caught his hand and said, 'Please don't go! Let's spend some more time together.'

He sat down, felt her release his hand and wondered about his immediate future. If he stayed any longer he wouldn't be able to control himself. Monica got up and holding his hand, guided him to the sofa, before sitting down next to him. She put her hands around him and looked into his eyes. Andy's instincts took over. He kissed the pink candies gently at first and then passionately as she played on. Her lips had a tremble of submission in them which gave him greater pleasure and he kissed her like he had always been her lover.

There was a knock on the door and the person outside had to use his knuckles twice for them to disengage. Andy felt embarrassed. She got back moments later and said it wasn't important.

She came close to him again. This time Andy moved away.

'This isn't right,' he told her. She nodded, her eyes hinting pain. But she moved back to her chair behind her desk and smiled. Andy got up, picked up his car keys and walked out of the office. She didn't stop him this time.

Andy reached his car and found a man leaning against it. It was time, he knew. He pointed a finger in one random direction, shook hands with him, felt the paper slide into his palms and got into the car as the man walked away. He drove away from Connaught Place for a kilo-metre or so and pulled to one side in a small, deserted parking alley. At first, Andy wondered if he really wanted to continue on this case. He battled with his conscience for a long time, till he finally remembered the oath he had taken when joining the Army. He took a deep breath and then gently unfolded the scrap of paper.

It took him less than five minutes to decipher that the old man now wanted him at a place called Baci in Sunder Nagar, at nine tonight. It was probably a restaurant, or perhaps an antique shop that was open till quite late. He drove home, looked for signs of trespass, and opened the lock. His living room smelt of stale food and his first reaction was that someone had broken into the house while he was away. He stiffened and walked around the sofas with caution. But the reason for the smell was something else and he found it in no time — a rotting peel of banana he had forgotten to discard.

His mind kept going back to the kiss and once again, he couldn't help imagining living with Monica as her sig-nificant other. Life could be so much fun. They could have sex whenever they wanted, and of course, they could take care of each other. Andy tried imagining how life would be with Monica, the two of them living together as lovers. Life could slow down a bit, but would turn a lot more wholesome.

He couldn't concentrate on the immediate meeting that evening. Was he falling in love? With the way things were, this was the last thing he had expected. It added a new dimension to the puzzle. Monica wanted him back in the magazine. He had told her that he was no longer interested in the case. But that was not the truth. The suspects had fled Tilakpur. Which meant he wasn't going back there any more. But the men who stayed at Tilakpur for two years had in all probability, developed a good network by now. There was no doubt about that. Gulabo had told them about South Block and Rashtrapati Bhawan in Delhi, and of Murud Janjira in Mumbai. Surely, the action had now shifted out of quaint Tilakpur.

Andy made up his mind. He didn't want to pursue the case any further. Life was far too safe and attractive with him going to the office, seeing Monica every day, and probably having a relationship with her. He knew that sooner or later, he would end up in bed with Monica. It was perhaps their combined destiny, and for the first time he challenged the thought of falling in love with a woman seven years older than him. There were so many couples with such age differences, some way more than seven. As he ate a banana from the bunch he had picked from under the building, he realized working with the magazine was far more interesting. He had his share of adventure in the army and as the government's occasional agent. No more, he thought with decisiveness, no more!

9

Andy heard the sound he was hoping not to. But this time he was better prepared. Before meeting Monica at the office, he had met one of his friends and borrowed his pistol. In a flash, Andy picked up the pistol in one hand, flipped the safety off and waited in the dark.

There was silence once again. He strained his ears. His living room was dark. He waited without switching the lights on. It was a ploy. If a visitor was planning an unscheduled visit, he would like to come in the dark. Because it meant either the occupant was away, or asleep. The silence continued. How long had the intruder been waiting outside the house? Was he there when Andy returned home three hours ago? There was no way of knowing.

Five minutes passed and his immediate surroundings

still remained silent. He could hear the distant sounds of vehicles on the road below. Was he imagining the whole thing? Could be. Andy cursed himself for letting the Tilakpur incident fray his nerves to such a degree that he felt detached from reality. Was he having delusions? Was he really so scared, enough to hallucinate? He knew such a condition came in almost all Army men's lives when facing adversity of gargantuan proportions for a long time.

But just then the sound came again, the gentlest of crushing of a tiny glass piece. There was someone outside the door, waiting, probably trying to open the lock without making any sound. Someone whose foot had once again crushed the small glass piece he had scattered outside the door. Andy's door was the last in the corridor with a dead end. So it couldn't be someone simply crossing to go over to the other side. There was no other side. Whoever was at the door was there because he had to be there. And he had been standing outside for longer than a few minutes now.

Andy could walk slowly to the door and see through the peep hole. But it was dangerous. Perhaps that's what the intruder wanted. But this time, he wouldn't make any mistakes. He rolled a half-filled plastic bottle towards the door. The water inside swooshed as the bottle moved, the sound very low. It stopped at the door with a thump. The water gurgled inside for a second longer. It was perfect and Andy waited.

He had imagined the intruder to push the door open. But whoever was outside was a professional. Two shots were fired. Two mild thuds. They punched clean holes through the wooden door and Andy could see two beams of the corridor light find its way inside. This was it, the moment Andy had been waiting for. He fired a single shot as soon as one of the holes got darker briefly. He heard a soft thud outside. The man had been hit! But with all that had happened so far, Andy knew better. Still holding the pistol in his hand and sweating, he called the building security guard on the intercom.

Then he waited, the pistol aimed straight at the door. After a few minutes he heard voices outside. They pressed the bell frantically and asked him to open the door. But Andy was too dazed and in any case, he wasn't taking any chances. There was every possibility that the society people might have also collaborated with the intruder to kill him. The people outside were now ramming themselves against the door, still yelling from outside for him to open. The latch came off after a few shoves and they came charging in.

Andy quickly hid the pistol under the cushion on the sofa. He knew he had killed the intruder — or at least injured him severely. Security guards and concerned residents stood around him now. They spoke to him together and he thought their voices were reaching him from under water. But the cloud cleared in no time.

They told him there was no one outside. Andy was shocked. He walked up and inspected the space just outside the door. There was no one, and no blood marks too. Had he really imagined the whole thing? No. The bullet marks — three of them, two by the intruder and one by him were still very much there as proof. He showed them to the guard and the neighbours and they looked concerned. One of them rationalized that these could have been there from before. Another said he had probably seen a bad dream.

Andy didn't pursue it any further. Slowly, they went their way and the door was closed. Andy pushed a chair under the door knob after he was alone. He didn't want to take any more chances. He felt uncomfortable in the house all by himself, with his enemies knowing about it. They had attempted to kill him and had removed the traces when they failed. It meant the intruder was not alone.

Andy now reconsidered his decision to abandon his intelligence assignment. The attack made it clear that he was too deep in this whole mess to back away now. The bad guys were after him too. Probably the same people who couldn't kill him at Gulabo's house owing to the delay in getting instructions from their handlers. They were now acting on revised instructions. He knew he had to get out of the house as his location had been compromised. If he saw Monica again, he would end up putting her in danger as well. Andy suddenly felt homeless and alone.

He packed quickly, his attention on the door all the time. He called the guard and walked out in his company. He had this uncanny feeling that he was being watched. It became necessary to leave his car behind as they might have either bugged it, or worse, planted a bomb in it. Andy immediately discounted the bomb theory. It would just raise the heat on them. Roads would be blocked and more police personnel pressed into action, compromising their primary focus. Yet it wasn't a risk he was prepared to take. Criminals were desperate people and they never followed exact rules or patterns.

Andy took the metro from the City Centre terminal station at Noida, not far from his house. It was ten minutes to nine and the train was deserted. No one paid any attention to him. Andy just waited patiently for his stop to arrive. The old man could wait for him. Half an hour later he got off at the Pragati Maidan station and slid into an autorickshaw right outside it.

Baci was tucked away in the middle of several shops selling antiques to foreign tourists. A narrow flight of stairs took him to a large restaurant, where a North-Eastern waitress smiled at him. He smiled back at her smile and looked around over her head. The old man was not anywhere to be seen. The lady guessed his predicament and told him that the restaurant had one more floor and he followed her to another level. Here, Japanese men and women occupied all the tables, save one where the old man was seated. The Japanese uncharacteristically talked loudly, wine and food in front of them.

Andy smiled at the old man without meaning it. He was sucked into this mess and the old man played a crucial role to keep him right there. Andy was the goat he was using for the tigers to walk into his trap.

The old man said hello and took a call on his cell phone, as Andy waited for him on the chair opposite. An unfinished glass of beer was on the table. A pleasant looking waiter came up and thrust a menu card in Andy's hands.

Suddenly, the old man shot to his feet. For a moment there, Andy was frightened seeing the look on his face. He was told they were leaving. Holding Andy's hands, the old man almost pulled him into the kitchen on the same floor. They passed several North-Eastern men and women who were slogging in the rather large kitchen, wearing white caps and aprons over jeans and T-shirts. An overpowering smell of flavours hung all over them. No one looked in their direction, as if they were invisible.

They came out on a terrace, where the old man finally paused and looked around cautiously. Then, on steadier legs they climbed down the stairs and came to a road behind the restaurant. The road was empty. They entered the small park and got out to the other side where a car waited for them. The old man started running to it, waved and urged Andy to get in.

The car rolled into the night as soon as they hobbled into the rear seat.

'What just happened?' Andy broke the silence, his body shaking with the sudden rush of excitement.

'You had a tail.' The old man didn't look at him. He was watching beyond the head of the driver.

'But...'

'Don't worry, not your fault. I should have been more careful. In any case, we're off their radar now. They'll keep wasting their time and energy waiting outside the restaurant thinking we're still inside.' The old man's voice was returning to the rhythm that Andy was used to hearing.

'I'm sorry.' Andy knew he could have been more careful. But he was late and his desperation to see the old man made him take short cuts. He cursed himself silently.

'They've killed Gulabo.' The old man's voice echoed like he was sitting in a well, not in a moving car.

'What?' Andy was shocked. The old man repeated himself, this time more slowly.

They sat in silence for a few more minutes till the driver pulled up in front of a café. Andy followed the old man inside and waited for him to order. Eggs and bread. And tea.

But his hunger had vanished. Gulabo was dead. He felt sad for her. She was a woman who had always been unhappy: married to an alcoholic, she had toiled her entire life in the hope for a better future for her daughter. Now she was gone before her daughter was settled.

'How?' He had to know.

'Her throat was slit, sometime this afternoon.'

Andy thought of the man outside his door. Was he the one who had killed her? In which case he had had his revenge.

'I was attacked too.' Andy told the old man in detail about the attack and how he was successful in fooling the attacker and killing him.

'But you couldn't fool them all the way, Captain. One of them followed you from your house to the restaurant.'

This was the second time the old man had referred to him by his rank.

'Don't call me Captain. I no longer work for the Army.' Andy's irritation showed in his voice, but Kapoor didn't care.

'Suit yourself. But I wouldn't mind if you called me Captain Kapoor.'

'You worked for the Army too?'

'Yes. For five years, just like you. Then I joined R&AW and now I'm on deputation to the Home Ministry for internal security.'

'It's an honour to meet you, Sir. But you're a Joint Secretary now and that's way up than a mere Captain. Why would you still like to be called a Captain?' Andy felt he knew the answer, but he had to be certain.

'There is nothing more honourable than the work we do in the Indian Army. Our brothers have fought wars, saved the integrity of this vast nation for more than six decades. The world thought India would disintegrate after independence...that there were too many differences – language, religions, race, caste, culture...But the Indian Army has played the most important role in keeping it all together. I would much rather be addressed as Captain than as a Joint Secretary.' The old man spoke with such passion that Andy felt the hair on his hands and legs rise. He could feel it as much as the old man.

The eggs and bread arrived. They ate in silence and washed it down with their teas.

Andy informed Kapoor about what Gulabo had told him. But he already knew it through Rohtas, the barman.

The old man asked Andy if he wanted to continue working for them. The choice was his. Andy said he would. They had tried to kill him and had taken Gulabo's life. He wasn't going to back down now.

There was pin-drop silence for a while. The old man finally said, 'The enemies are within striking distance and a major terrorist attack seems imminent. It could be Mumbai or Delhi.'

They discussed some more. The old man shared other snippets of information and they reassessed the situation in the light of these revelations. A possible scenario began to emerge:

The sleeper cell at Tilakpur was created for surveillance purposes. South Block and Rashtrapati Bhawan were the probable targets. The former housed the Prime Minister's office and the Defence Ministry, while the President, the supreme commander of the three Defence services, resided in the latter. So they were targeting the Defence. The same Defence, Andy and the old man once worked for. The very Defence that had saved the nation so many times in the past. Mumbai was probably a conduit point and the beach at Murud was possibly being used as a landing point. This naturally meant that the sea route was essential in this plot.

The scenario was based on the observations of Andy, the various intelligence organizations involved, and their collective analysis. It could have its inaccuracies, but at the moment it looked like a fair assumption, and also the only possible lead for them to follow.

And then came something that took the wind out of Andy's chest.

'We have our doubts about Monica.'

Andy thought he lacked air to breathe. He felt choked, as if someone was strangling him.

The old man continued, 'We've been watching her for some time now. We were watching when you were with her this evening.'

Did they watch them kissing? Andy felt naked. Was there a hidden camera in Monica's room?

'We have her on camera. But don't worry. I understand that she's an attractive woman, she's just too hard to resist. But remember, she might be using you.'

Andy felt relieved that they hadn't gone the full distance in the evening. Or now the old man, and who knows how many others, would know the size of his dick.

'Do you have any conclusive evidence? What can she possibly gain by helping terrorists destroy her own country?' She seemed too innocent for such elaborate schemes. He recalled how her lovers had used and ditched her. He thought deeply. It might be true. There was no doubt that she adored him. But was it she who asked those people at Tilakpur to spare his life when they caught up with him. She seemed completely shaken when she had visited him in the hospital. He also remembered how fidgety she was the day she had sent him to Tilakpur, chewing the end of her pencil. But this afternoon she was cool and relaxed. Perhaps she was certain that he wouldn't be involved with this any more.

'I'm afraid we're not a hundred percent sure...yet. But there are inferences drawn, which lead us to assume the worst. Look, I'm sorry...In any case, she's too old!'

Andy didn't like the old man's telling him which woman to love. He bloody well knew what was good for him. He got up and walked away into the night. The old man called after him and caught up soon. He was out of breath. Andy felt his hand rest on his shoulder and he stopped.

'I know I have no business interfering in your personal matters. I'm sorry! I won't talk about this again. But you have to promise me that you'll be careful.'

Andy nodded and walked away towards his new destination. Mumbai. The old man had explained to him in detail about his new assignment in the financial capital of the country. No written notes, just like when he was sent to Tilakpur. It was all verbal: contacts, rules of engagement, scenarios, SOPs, etc.

It was getting hot now. The bets were all off. Andy was now in the thick of it. Things were going to get a lot uglier and Andy had to be prepared for it.

10

Andy liked Mumbai. The weather was cleaner than Delhi, the mornings clearer as the sea sucked out the pollution each night, the men minded their own business, their focus unwavering as they scurried between homes, meetings and offices. The women were noticeably fashionable and pretty, blossoming without the men's attention perhaps, something which Andy always thought was a pity. He believed Delhi boys and Mumbai girls were the best combination ever. But the Dilliwallas and the Mumbaikars loathed each other.

Andy landed at Chhatrapati Shivaji International airport in an Indigo flight on a cool night. He flew economy, though he itched to travel executive with the government money he now had. After all, he was entitled to a little luxury and he sure as hell could use the rest. And the government wasn't paying him any overtime either. But in the end he chose economy more out of habit than anything else.

Mumbai is huge — a megacity that was never intended. Created by joining seven islands, Mumbai is a mass of reclaimed land that was passed by the Portuguese to the British as dowry in colonial times. An accidental hub today, it attracts people from far and wide. On Mumbai's south, Arabs, Whites and Africans rub shoulders with the Iranis, Parsis, Gujaratis and the naval sailors in crew cuts. It was here that Andy's black and yellow taxi was headed at ten at night.

The driver took the Worli Sea Link and in less than twenty minutes, they were flying past the Haji Ali mosque. But Peddar Road, even at a late hour like this, had cars queuing up like snails on a highway. The driver hurled a few abuses in a thick Bihari accent. Andy asked him how bad it was being a Bihari in Mumbai. The driver turned pale slightly, but continued cursing until the taxi reached the 'queen's necklace' or Marine Drive, as it is more popularly known. The driver now cruised at almost 100 kmph and seemed happy.

Andy didn't spare the government when it came to deciding on a place to stay. As if he'd returned home after winning a war, a burly Sikh in a cummerbund saluted Andy and held the taxi door open for him to get down. This was the first time he was visiting the Trident after the deadly terrorist attack in 2008. He went through security and walked in smiling wildly.

Once in his room on the 14th floor that overlooked the bay, he thought about his next course of action. Andy had checked-in under a false name with the fake identity provided by Kapoor. 'Now that they know your name, they might be watching you,' he had said in a brief message.

Andy took a therapeutic hot shower for ten minutes, dressed in fresh denims and a white half-sleeved linen shirt and went to the bar. It was ten-fifty. There were a few men and women speaking rather loudly, laughing at each other's slightest display of humour. A typical late night bar scene in any hotel in the world. No one noticed him come in and sit on a stool by the counter, except a tired looking waitress who smiled at him warmly. He ordered a large 100 Pipers on the rocks, instead of his Old Monk rum — a new drink for a new identity.

Andy called Hakim using the new chip that came with the identity papers. As the phone continued to ring, Andy sipped his whisky. The call went unanswered and he decided to try again after a few minutes. When on his third drink, he was finally able to get through to a man who said he might not be Hakim, but was still willing to meet him at Colaba at midnight. He sounded weird on the phone and Andy's attention sensed the hesitation of a double cross in his voice. He knew he had to be careful.

From the hotel, he started walking towards Colaba on the Madame Cama Road, with the local ministers' houses on his right and the Mantralaya, the state secretariat, on his left. Scores of policemen in khaki walked about munching *vada pav*, their favourite midnight snack. He arrived at Café Royal, opposite the police headquarters in Colaba, at the stroke of midnight. The manager walked him in and he chose a table for two near the wall. He sat waiting and asked for a cola, careful not to drink too much or his senses would be sullied. Brightly painted portraits of Bill Clinton and Marilyn Monroe looked at him; the former his studious best with empathetic eyes —Andy was reminded of Monica Lewinsky — and the latter struggling to keep her skirt down, her eyes helpless and the lips a perfect pout of invitation.

Fifteen minutes later a man walked into the café and looked around uncertainly.

Andy called out, 'Hakim!'

The man was about sixty and sported a sparse beard. His forehead was darker, suggesting his accustomed and regular prayers. He was wearing trousers and a T-shirt which was too loose for him, the kind of clothes he wasn't used to wearing. When he shook his hand, Andy realized the man's hand was trembling. It also left his palm wet.

'You shouldn't have called out my name so loudly.' He was constantly looking at the entrance instead of Andy.

There was a shadow outside and Andy was quick to realize the danger, as Hakim's mouth opened wide.

Instinctively, Andy punched Hakim hard on his nose.

He screamed in reflex, as though he was dying. The manager came running and they were soon surrounded by waiters in seconds. In all the hullabaloo, one of the waiters tripped and the action brought the others crashing down on them, like footballers jumping on each other after scoring a goal.

Andy made his way through the heap of bodies as they scrambled back to their feet and dashed for the entrance. He saw the shadow at a slight distance from him. The distance from the entrance proved to Andy something he already knew — the man was uncertain if he should run away or watch what happened next. By now two policemen patrolling nearby, were heading for the café.

In the end, seeing Andy rush out, the man decided to run. He was a large man and Andy was sure he would catch up with him soon. The man ran towards the High Court and Andy followed him, the distance between them reducing faster and faster. Suddenly, a car appeared out of nowhere and the man jumped into it and it dissolved in the night mist as Andy stopped and watched after it, out of breath. All this happened too quickly for him.

Andy returned to Café Royal. The policemen were asking Hakim questions in a strong Marathi accent. Andy decided to help the poor man, even if it came with the doubt of a double cross. Help is help and Andy knew it should be treated as such. It took him ten minutes to send the policemen walking back.

'Who was that man outside?' Andy asked him after they were alone and the restaurant got back to business once again.

'I don't know. But for the last one week I have seen strange people watching me all the time. I'm very scared, Sir.' His voice sounded like someone who was convinced he wouldn't survive for long. Andy was told that Hakim had been helping the police and intelligence agencies for the past ten years. These things came with considerable risks and Andy felt his time might have run out.

'Please send your family to a safe place.' Andy decided to pull the carpet under him. It was a blow for sure. The man's eyes rolled and he nearly fainted. He was being told that he should now prepare to die.

'I thought the government would eliminate these men.' He was shaking, a cola glass exhaling bubbles sitting untouched in front of him.

'If only you act brave. If you panic like a pigeon, the cat will pounce on you and devour you. Don't close your eyes. If you think your life is in danger, their lives are in danger too. And everyone else's in Mumbai city if the enemies have their way. We have to stop them. Your enemy and the nation's enemy are the same, Hakim. It is the question of who strikes first.'

Hakim nodded and finally decided to turn to the cola

for relief. He finished it in one go and banged the glass on the table rather noisily. Andy thought the man was taking control of himself and smiled.

'What do you have for me?' Andy pressed for more information.

'Murud Janjira.'

'What's that?' Andy had heard the name from Gulabo and had seen it in Kapoor's evaluation too.

'It's an unmanned fort on an island about 180 kilometres south of Mumbai.'

'What's at Murud?'

'Explosives, I think.'

Hakim got up after this and left the restaurant, as if he suddenly remembered something important.

Andy paid for both of them. From the café he walked to the deserted Gateway of India, a hundred metres away. The air was cooler than he had hoped and he felt the shiver. Mumbai was never cold enough for anyone to use woollens, but at this moment, late at night, Andy wished he had something warmer on. He watched the ships in the distance anchored inside the harbour, their decks lit brightly. Small boats bobbed in and out of the waves and their lights shimmered. He turned and watched the Taj hotel with awe. It had been restored after the fire and bombings by the terrorists a couple of years ago. Now it looked grand, as it always did.

He considered the terrorists who had sailed in fishing boats from Karachi, braving the rough Arabian Sea for three gruelling days, their peanut-sized brains bleached white for a guaranteed seat in heaven. Were these the same people who were now planning to replicate such an attack? Send more brainwashed fools? But fools could also do a lot of damage, like they did the previous time.

Andy took a taxi and asked the driver to take him to Churchgate station. Once settled inside the cab, he turned around in his seat and was proved right. There was another taxi that was taking exactly the same turns as his. He asked the driver to stop and watched the other taxi cross him and go ahead. The man in the passenger seat was small and stared at him as he overtook Andy's stalled taxi. The man didn't look scared. His eyes were hard and seemed to have a deadly purpose.

Andy paid the driver, asked him to keep the change and got down. The taxi that had followed him was about fifty metres ahead. It too had stopped, as if waiting for Andy to make the first move. Andy crossed the road, running, and stood behind a building, his breath halted. He was under a banyan tree, hiding amidst its dangling roots.

Andy pulled himself up on the rope-like-roots, just like he used to practise in the Academy and settled on a low branch. The leaves gave him the perfect cover. He waited.

Andy knew that the man had seen him head in this direction. A few minutes later he saw him emerge from behind the building. The man was quick on his feet and walked on his toes. He was a professional. But so was Andy.

He jumped in front of the man. The trick was to shock him. Before the man could recover from the surprise, Andy hit him under his jaw and followed it with another quick punch into his solar plexus. As the man wavered on his feet, about to fall, Andy laid a thick, heavy punch right on the stomach. The man was small and he flung to the pavement, a pistol falling from his hand. Andy took two quick steps and kicked the gun out of reach. He then dragged his attacker behind the tree quickly. Sometimes, a tail carried another tail for safety. Professionals do this. It has two purposes. One, the second tail can help if the first ran into trouble. Like now. Second, the tails can switch back and forth, making it difficult for the man being followed to be sure if he was indeed being followed.

The man was whimpering now, blood trickling from the sides of his mouth. Andy was sure he had caused an internal injury and the man would drown in his own blood if he wasn't taken to a hospital soon. But he couldn't care less. This man was an enemy of the nation.

'Who are you?'

The man looked at him and smiled through his blood-soaked teeth. Andy was confused till he saw the froth oozing out of his mouth. He was dying and he was happy for it. The man shuddered and slumped to the ground, dead. Once again, Andy was surprised by the ability of those who brainwashed them. The man at his feet had just swallowed a cyanide capsule. He chose death over revealing anything about his bosses. Andy punched the air in frustration.

He quickly ran through the man's pockets and removed a thin wallet with a few hundred rupees and a mobile phone. He checked the phone for messages. There were none. He checked the number logs and found one number that was called twice. The rest of the caller log was empty. He pocketed both, the wallet and the phone. Then he picked up the pistol and pocketed that too.

Andy waited a slight distance away, hoping to spot the second tail. But none came. After half an hour, he resumed his walk towards the hotel. He wanted to keep the pistol, but knew that the hotel security wouldn't let him through. Still, it was worth trying. If he was caught he could call the number the old man had given him for immunity in such cases.

At two in the morning, the hotel's security staff just looked at him with a tired smile. Andy had shoved the pistol into his socks. He slid his phone and wallet into the container lined with velvet, to be carried through the detector and smiled at the young man who was about to frisk him. The man ran his hands till Andy's waist and let him through. Andy collected his phone and wallet and walked in. It was only then that Andy realized that he was very tired.

Once in the confines of his room, he felt assured of his safety. Yet, he instinctively checked the bathroom. It was empty. Andy took a hot water shower and switched on the television to keep himself distracted for some time. In less than ten minutes he fell asleep without even knowing about it.

But Andy had missed the second tail. It was very much there, keeping in the shadows. It saw him jump and over-power the man. After he was gone, this tail, a big man who moved like a giant monkey, floated near the dead man. He smiled and said a small prayer. There was no remorse. The dead man had departed for heaven, where he was to follow soon.

He called a number and spoke briefly. There was a need to fortify their defences, he was told. The two of them had failed to execute their orders. He assured his boss that the situation was under control. The monkey-man knew where Andy stayed and therefore, he started walking towards the hotel. He even knew the floor and the room number.

He reached Marine Drive and sat on the parapet, ca-sually, like a passer-by would. There were manmade boul-ders down below on which the Arabian Sea was crashing violently. The same Arabian Sea that was to bring in reinforcements. The same Arabian Sea that brought warriors the last time. But he wasn't aware of the plan this time. He always minded his own business, which was to kill his target, whoever it was. He never asked questions.

The monkey-man moved his head up, counted the floors and began staring at the room in which he thought Andy slept. He was patient, the virtue necessary for killers. He had more experience than his partner who was overpowered, and now dead. He began to wait, totally at ease, humming a Hindi film song, his eyes stuck to one particular window many floors up.

11

akim was walking fast. His chawl was tucked right behind Bhindi Bazaar. At one at night, there were few people on the road, though many were asleep on the narrow pavements.

He was worried. Really worried. The incidents of the night had frightened him out of his wits. In ten years as a police informant he had never experienced trouble. In fact, he was so happy with the easy money it earned him that he was thinking of pushing his eighteen-year-old son into it after a couple of years.

Hakim's job as an informant was simple. He just had to keep his eyes and ears open. At shops in the busy Crawford Market, at local bars near the Mazgaon docks, at the mosque in Kalbadevi, and at antique shops in Chor Bazaar. Whenever he had something interesting, he would go to a predetermined place and pass on the information to someone from the police who would be waiting for him in plain clothes. But during the past few months something had gone wrong and his identity had been compromised.

He cursed his newest wife who insisted on buying an LCD television soon after marriage. The neighbours had seen the television arrive and she had boasted that it cost forty thousand rupees. Forty thousand, she had repeated in a loud voice for everyone to hear. One of them asked where she got the money from as her husband only managed odd jobs to make ends meet and had three wives and ten children to feed at home.

'He works for the government and they pay him good money,' his new wife had contradicted their opinion.

She told this to Hakim the same night, minutes after they had a satisfying sex session. He lay next to her as he heard this, panting, the sweat rolling on the sides from his dark forehead. He knew that this was a big blunder. Right then and there, he knew this could cost him his life.

He pleaded with her right at that moment. 'Don't discuss my job with others in the future!'

She seemed surprised, but agreed in the end. Hakim found her so attractive that he couldn't get angry with her. He wanted to shout, twist her ears, and slap her. But he simply couldn't. It added to his frustration.

Hakim's new wife was raised at a small village near Aligarh town in Uttar Pradesh. Her name was Heena and she was ambitious. A year ago, when he met her father and expressed his desire to marry her, the man had demanded to know how he would support his daughter as he had no steady job. Hakim had hesitated for a few seconds, but in the end, overcome by the raw appeal of a seventeen-year-old bride, he boasted that he worked for the government and they paid him a lot of money. For the *nikah*, he had offered a sum of ten lakh rupees as *meher* and Heena, along with her father and relatives, was very happy. The marriage was solemnized a week later. She was excited that she was moving to Mumbai, the city of Bollywood, the city of wealth, the city of dreams.

Heena always wanted to be a dancer. She knew she was beautiful. The boys at her village had made it easy for her to get this impression. They were always following her, singing songs to impress her, asking her to accompany them to Aligarh city to watch movies. Once she realized the perks of being beautiful, her ambition skyrocketed. She would ask her lovers to get her beauty creams, clothes and cosmetics. In return, she hung out with them and sometimes even allowed them to touch her. Before she was sixteen, Heena had broken off relationships with three boyfriends, as she realized they didn't have any money left to spend on her. Her requirement was only money, because with it, she knew, she could stay desirable all her life. She liked getting the attention of men.

When Hakim visited her home and someone told her that he was from Mumbai, she liked him immediately.

His age did not matter because he was someone who had money and lived in the right place. She was overcome with the craving to go with him and make a new future. She already loved Mumbai, even though she had never been there. She knew Mumbai had colour, a beautiful sea and lots of money. When she heard that Hakim had promised her father a sum of ten lakh rupees as *meher*, she was ecstatic. With that kind of money she could buy her own house in Mumbai and live happily.

Looking at Hakim's eyes and seeing the way he looked hungrily at her bosom, she immediately knew what he really wanted. It would be easy. By now she had slept with many men. Hakim was her way out and all she needed to give him in return was her body. She married him without any further thought. He would take her to Mumbai with dignity and give her money to be happy. She made up her mind to stay with him for six months. It would be enough for her to figure out how things worked in Mumbai. After that she could start dancing in films. Soon, she was to be a huge star.

When Heena reached Mumbai, her dreams were shattered. Her rich husband was a pauper here. She had to live in a stinking *chawl* and share two small rooms with two other women and ten children. The women were much older than her and chewed *paans* endlessly. They didn't talk to her and the children were aged from six to eighteen. After winning Hakim's confidence and becoming his favourite wife with whom he spent all his nights now, she informed him one night about her plans to dance in the movies. She couldn't succeed. No matter how hard she tried to please him, Hakim said he would never give her permission to pursue her dreams. He said, 'Dancing in the movies is a cheap thing to do.' That made her dislike Hakim to a degree that she started thinking of ways to get rid of him.

One afternoon she met Imran. She had gone to the hand-pump in front of the chawl to fetch water for her bath. He winked at her and she smiled.

Then she walked up to him and said, 'Don't you know that I am married?'

He laughed and said, 'Yes, I know. I have been watching you from the time you arrived as a bride six months ago. But I am surprised... what are you doing spoiling your life with a haggard like Hakim?'

Imran said he was twenty-three and had a job that gave him fifty thousand each month. He said she was beautiful and had a great voice. His lips were dry when he said this, and she watched him lick them again and again to keep them moist.

Heena looked at him closely. He had green eyes, a wide jaw and an athletic, six feet body. He wore a shirt and its top button was open. It fell loosely on blue jeans. His teeth were white when he smiled and his hands were long and powerful. She wanted to be held in his arms, she wanted to be told that she could be a dancer.

'I want to be a dancer in the movies. Can you help me?'

Imran smiled and said, 'Yes. I know a few people in the film industry. I can talk to them. Yes, we can make you a dancer in the movies.'

That evening, she quietly slipped into his small room and gave herself whole-heartedly to him. She knew he would get addicted to her charm.

One morning, after Hakim left home for a few hours, Imran asked her to join him in his room. There was another man there. He asked her to imitate Rekha's dancing steps from the movie *Umrao Jaan*. It was a test, Imran told her. Heena had practised this dance several times. It was one of her favourites. She sang herself and danced. The mouths of the men were still open after she finished. The man said she had great potential and he would get a good offer for her soon. After he left, she looked at Imran and smiled. He jumped on her and made love. He kept saying it felt like having sex with a real actress. Heena was overjoyed.

Imran came back with the news a week later that she could dance in a group that was being led by one of the top Hindi film actresses. Heena was wild with happiness. But Hakim was a barrier. She couldn't tell him and the opportunity passed. It broke her heart. After that day, whatever

Imran wanted to know about her husband she told him without any hesitation. She noted down the numbers he called while he was in the bathroom and passed it on to Imran. She had no idea why Imran wanted these details, but she did it all the same. She knew she was bringing some danger to her husband, but now she didn't care less. She already had Imran in her hands. He was rich, young and crazy for her.

So it wasn't Hakim's third wife, Heena's declaring to her neighbours that the television was for forty thousand or that he worked for the government that got him in trouble. It was her association with Imran that doomed Hakim's future. Imran passed all these details to the right people in exchange for money.

As Hakim neared his home, he felt death closing in on him. He regretted getting married to Heena, and yet he wanted to return soon into her arms. His other wives were useless. They had become flaccid and unattractive. But Heena was not like that. She smelt sweet and provided him pleasure as he rocked her gently during the nights, her moans disturbing his other wives in the adjacent room. It heightened his pleasure. They deserved this. Had they taken better care of themselves and of him, he wouldn't have acquired another wife.

Hakim could see his *chawl* now and it drowned his worries by half. In the *chawl* waited Heena, his wife, the mother of his future children, and the hope of his old age.

He smiled.

Something bit his back. Before he could turn, he felt it tear. Hakim fell facedown. He felt wetness inside him and within seconds he couldn't breathe properly. Am I dying, he thought? But there was no pain and he wasn't able to move his hands to get up.

He noticed a pool of blood that had formed under him. It was ballooning away from him, an overhead street-light reflecting in it. Slowly his vision began to blur and someone came and stood over him. The person looked like Heena, but he wasn't sure till he heard her voice. There was no panic as he heard her say, 'Why didn't you allow me to dance in the movies?'

Hakim closed his eyes. Perhaps he should have allowed her to do as she wished. It surprised him that not giving his permission for her to dance would cost him his life. He wasn't angry. Heena had given him numerous pleasurable moments. She was his wife, his favourite wife. Hakim opened his mouth to speak, but his eyes rolled over. He was dead.

Two men stood over him. Hakim had imagined Heena in his final moments. One of the men had a big knife with a crooked tip. Blood dripped from it. They looked at each other and smiled. The mission was accomplished and now it was time to lose themselves for a few months. They walked over to their Royal Enfield Bullet 350 cc and kicked the 20 horse power engine to life. *Dhuk, dhuk, dhuk.*

They vanished into the night.

Monica was with her boss at his Chhatarpur farmhouse outside Delhi, on the way to Gurgaon. The boss seemed relaxed, his back resting on an easy chair. A soft pillow was tucked under his head and his rotund body was covered in a pashmina shawl. A gentle smile played on his lips. Monica sat on the edge of a similar chair, upright and unsmiling.

They were seated in the lawn, the sun right above them. The lawn was well kept, and flowers — Dianthuses, Gerberas and Marigolds — smiled at them from the sides. The ten feet walls that encircled the two-acre farmhouse kept them secluded from the world outside. A Labrador moved about like a detective at work, smelling grass, its nose wet with dew.

Monica was worried that her state of mind showed to people around her. Why had he summoned her? Her boss looked at her, his smile widening. He sank further in the easy chair. For the world he was a pious man. But Monica, who knew his ambition, thought otherwise. She had been working with him for four years now and it was enough for her to understand him to a great extent. Her boss wanted to be the king maker — in politics and in business. He had money and influence. The world knew him by the name of Krishna Bedi or 'KB Sahib'.

KB had a plan for every situation. Not just a plan, he also had plans B and C if things went out of hand. He was organized, meticulous, unmarried and had no vices. He had never loved a woman. His only motivation was money and he wanted more and more of it. KB knew money and power were two sides of the same coin. If he wanted to earn more money, he would need more power. And in democracy, power belonged to the people. Therefore, he wanted the people to be on his side and he had been working on a plan for the past three years to get them behind him.

In the Forbes list of the richest in the world, KB was ranked 10th. In Asia he was second and in India he was the richest man. At fifty, he knew people behaved according to the stimulus. With the money and influence he had, KB could make the people of the second most populous nation happy or angry at will. He was their stimulus. He controlled the minds of the people and therefore both, the future of the nation, and the future of his empire, was firmly in his hands.

KB thought the ruling party at the Centre was like a headless chicken. The Americans had cut its head off and the Europeans had thrown it away, and in the mayhem, everyone was having a free hand. Markets were being opened up in the areas he monopolized and his fiefdom was being challenged. There were white dogs everywhere now in India, the Americans and the Europeans, eating his pound of flesh and snarling at him.

Many of his business deals were stuck due to the policies of the current government. He now wanted a puppet government at the Centre, a government which could give him a small window of time and he could have his way.

His interest ranged from petrochemicals, real estate and telecommunications, to media and entertainment. KB owned the *New Delhi Today*. It was the mouthpiece which ran stories that favoured his scheme of things.

To overcome his hurdles, KB had made a brief plan. It was his most ambitious plan yet and he christened it 'Dirty Bomb for Dirty Politics'. As always he was discreet about it. But for any plan to be successful, he also knew efficient minds were crucial. He had therefore, selected his collaborator, one Kismet Khan, a Pakistan-based politician-cum-businessman, very carefully.

Kismet Khan hated the Americans as much as KB. He hated them for sullying the minds of the Pakistani and Afghanistan politicians and killing his brothers and sisters in the North West Frontier Province (NWFP). He hated them for diluting his religion, as Hollywood movies were a bad influence and available inexpensively everywhere in Pakistan. In these movies, women wore bikinis and danced hanging from poles in front of lecherous men. Men consumed drugs and were never shown praying. These infidels were making his men infidels too. He had enough of them. He wanted to do something about this, to fix this growing problem in his country, but nobody seemed interested. So he wanted to take the responsibility upon himself to teach them a lesson.

When Kismet suggested that a big bomb was the best way to teach the Americans a lesson, it was music for KB's ears. An Improvised Explosive Device, an IED that was packed with something more than the usual ingredients would create the right degree of panic. KB needed no further convincing. He knew this would bring the government down on its knees.

KB wanted the Americans to get scared of doing business with India and run away. Now with the help of Kismet Khan, he finally had the perfect recipe.

Undoubtedly KB and Kismet Khan were driven by a common enemy — America. But what could that special material be? It didn't take them too long to figure it out.

When KB said the ingredients should be nuclear material, Kismet Khan jumped at the idea.

He said, 'I'll provide all the support that's required. I have access to the Pakistani government and the Pakistani government also wants someone in India they can trust.'

'The bomb is just a threat and it will only be used as a last resort.'

KB wanted to tell the government that he had control over the bomb when he placed his demands on the table. If the government didn't relent, the bomb would be detonated and thousands would die. In its aftermath the ruling party would be thrown out of power for letting it happen. Through his magazine and the other media channels he controlled/influenced, he would spread the news that it was an intentional plan of the government to mislead the people and stay in power. With paid content on the internet becoming the order of the day, he could use his websites to fully spread the news amongst the youth. There would be *dharnas* and strikes and the nation would be paralyzed for trusting the ruling party for so many years.

So far it had been going good for KB. They were making the bomb at a secluded place and no one had noticed their progress. Until one day, when Monica had sent a reporter named Andy Karan to Tilakpur.

KB had spared Andy's life twice, because he didn't want the entire attention of the police and the intelligence at Tilakpur. But his patience was wearing thin.

'Monica, tell me more about this guy, this Andy Karan, your correspondent...' KB looked at her, the smile in place, like an ornament.

'Andy has been with us for three years now. He was earlier with the Army. He has dropped the investigation at Tilakpur like you asked me to.' Monica stuck to the very basic facts.

His eyes had a mysterious spark as if he liked what she was telling him. KB scratched his beard. 'Can you tell me where this Andy chap is at the moment?'

Monica was somewhat surprised. Her boss, who had never asked her about the magazine's staff till date, was taking too much interest in Andy. First, he wanted the investigation dropped; then he wasn't concerned about the falling readership of the magazine and now he was keen to know more about Andy just because he had gone to Tilakpur. Something seemed amiss, but she maintained an innocent face.

'This Andy character is dangerous. He's not telling you everything. I suspect his intentions.' He searched for a reaction in Monica's eyes.

He handed her a packet. Monica quickly opened it and a few pictures slipped out on the glass table. It had pictures of Andy talking to an old man in a restaurant.

'I like your integrity, Monica. But he is double crossing us. He is not working for the magazine alone. I think he's hand in glove with some really bad people. Do you know where he is at this moment?'

She shook her head. She really had no idea.

'Mumbai.'

She felt a jab in her chest and tried to speak, but couldn't. Andy had not paid any heed to her requests to stay away. She felt sad. She had no idea what KB would do to him now.

Monica began to hate KB. She found herself taking Andy's side all of a sudden. He was doing something worthy, fighting for the truth, fighting without greed. But she still couldn't figure out where KB fitted into all this.

She thought of asking him, but before she could make up her mind, KB waved her away. Monica rose without a word and walked towards the gates. The Labrador followed her throughout, as did the gaze of KB, who appeared to study the swing of her hips for a signal. He was no longer smiling.

12

Andy woke up four hours before Monica's conversation with her boss, in Mumbai. Through the window of his room the first thing he saw was an aquamarine sea. It was eight and the sun had just crept out. A gentle westerly swell brought the sea to a hungry coast, where it rose in waves and crashed playfully on it. He felt rested and stretched his hands over his head. Fourteen floors below on the Marine Drive pavement, morning walkers and joggers went about purposefully, peanut and *bhelpuri* sellers at their heels, hoping for an early morning sale. It was a typical Mumbai morning.

But Andy wasn't in a typical situation. Hakim had mentioned Murud Janjira and explosives to him at Café Royal last night. There were people shadowing Hakim and they had watched the two of them meet. He had killed one, while the others had managed to escape. Andy wasn't sure if they knew where he lived.

He wanted to meet the Police Commissioner before heading to Murud Janjira. Mr Kapoor had already told Andy that no one else knew about his visit to Mumbai. He had explained that there were moles everywhere in the police department and his life would be in danger if they knew about him. But he had met Hakim last night and apparently they already knew of his existence.

His forehead furrowed in deep thought, Andy paced in the room. Ten minutes later he packed. Staying in the same room for longer than a day could mean trouble. As it is, he doubted the hotel's security and vigilance. Just the previous night he had easily smuggled a pistol inside the hotel. Andy quickly showered and got ready. After he was done, he plugged the bathtub and flooded the bathroom.

He reached the reception and said his bathroom had flooded. The staff apologized and asked if he wanted to change rooms and he agreed. He was put in a room a floor below. He went back to his room and collected his small bag. Depositing it into the new room he realized that he was hungry and descended to the restaurant on the ground floor, the pistol carefully hidden in his socks.

He ate slowly, chewing mouthfuls and washing it down with fresh orange juice. After he was done, he settled with the newspaper and asked for a glass of milk. There wasn't anything in the newspaper that interested him, but to keep his mind away from the moment he read through a few pages. After half an hour, setting it aside, he ate the final course — his favourite, bananas. Andy felt energetic and refreshed.

He walked out into the sun and checked behind him. There wasn't anyone who seemed even remotely interested in him. He found a phone booth and called Mr Kapoor's number. The numbers from outside to inside, just the way the old man had said he liked to work. He was smiling as he recalled the phone number, deciphering it on the basis of his cell phone keypad. All he could hear was a recorded message. It was strange. He waited near the pay phone for a few minutes, hoping for it to come alive. But the line stayed silent. He tried a second time and was greeted with the same recorded message. Weird. He then thought of calling Monica, but immediately decided against it.

At a distance of about fifty metres from the pay phone, the monkey-man watched him with his ever alert eyes. He had not slept a wink, yet he looked fresh like he'd come back from a vacation. He curled his long and powerful fingers in anticipation. The monkey-man liked strangling his victims with his bare hands. Many of his victims now lay dead as testimony to that fact.

As Andy walked towards Police Headquarters in Colaba, the monkey-man stayed behind him. Andy often turned to check if he was being followed, but by now the pavements were full of Mumbaikars headed to their offices in Flora Fountain, Ballard Pier or Colaba. The Mumbai local trains brought thousands of them and in the crowd he obviously couldn't make out if he was being followed. But to be doubly sure, he broke into a run and turned left before Jahangir Art Gallery, crossed Lion Gate, inside which naval ships lay docked, and approached Police HQ. He waited at the reception, deposited his pistol for safety as the jaw of the man who took it from him dropped, and was escorted ten minutes later into another room where the Police Commissioner joined him immediately. They were left alone.

Andy smiled and extended his hand. The Police Commissioner heard his story, but dropped a bombshell after he had finished. He said he didn't know any Mr Kapoor and no one had called him about this meeting.

Andy was exasperated.

'Sir, I need some back-up for Murud Janjira.' Without intending, it sounded like he was pleading.

'I'm sorry... I don't have people to act on whims. The Prime Minister is visiting Mumbai tomorrow and my hands are full. I have a very large city to protect. Just because someone has mentioned the name of a place, I can't send my men on a wild good chase compromising the home front. Maybe, that's what they want us to do.' He got up and extended his hands. The meeting was over.

Andy walked out empty-handed. He found another

phone booth and called Mr Kapoor again. Still no reply. Ideas began to form in his mind. Did Mr Kapoor really work for Indian intelligence? He had never met him at his office. The money that had been deposited into his account could have been anyone's. Was Andy spending dirty money, not the government's? He began to sweat.

The time was just after twelve and Andy felt desperate. He called Monica. She answered after the first ring.

Before he could say anything, he heard Monica speak, her voice bordering on panic, 'Andy, I met KB yesterday... you know, the one who owns the magazine. He was very keen to know everything about you. I think it has something to do with the Tilakpur investigation. I don't have a good feeling about this. He also knows that you're in Mumbai...are you?'

Andy didn't answer. His mind was busy, trying to connect the dots.

'Please be careful...promise me you will!'

'Don't worry about me, Monica. I'll be fine... I wanted to say something, but don't know how to say it...' And then he hung up. Monica's voice had diluted some of his anxiety. But it took him just a few seconds to get back.

Andy turned in the nick of time. The monkey-man was about to reach for his neck. He had moved like a snake despite his heavy body, and was now within inches from him. Andy kicked him in the groin — the only way to bring a giant to his knees. He growled and his eyes turned rounder. Before he could breathe, Andy kicked him again.

The man collapsed like a pack of cards. Leaving him right there he ran out of the old building passageway and into the sun. Hundreds of faces stared directly at him and Andy thought each of them was his enemy. His brain had stopped working. He ran, took random turns till the time he was out of breath and nearly fainted. He leaned on a streetlight and slumped down slowly, his back sliding against it.

Andy's life was in danger. Monica, without her knowing, appeared to be in danger too. That put the two of them on the same side. Mr Kapoor seemed to have disappeared and the Police Commissioner hadn't heard of him. Andy felt short-changed. Who was the enemy and where was he? He felt trapped in a computer game with virtual enemies, who had no emotions; but they could kill. And if he killed them, they didn't know the pain because they never existed in reality. Everything around him was virtual.

He thought of the futility of going to Murud Janjira in the present situation. It could well be a trap, where they could get rid of him easily. Just throw him in the water for the sharks to feast. Andy wondered how he would taste.

Suddenly, something hit his chest with a mild thud. Andy looked down. A tiny red dot had appeared on his white shirt. As he watched it blot and get bigger, he knew what it meant. So they had caught up with him at last. His running was of no use now. He had failed. The bad guys had won. He looked up at the sky and it seemed bluer than usual. He was losing his vision and fell to the ground. Pedestrians began closing in on him, pointing their fingers and speaking earnestly to each other. The crowd around him began to swell. The last thing he heard was the police siren.

Murud Janjira is an island fort off the coast of Maharashtra. It is located about half a kilometre from a small fishing village called Murud in the Raigard district of the state. One of the strongest marine forts in India, it was first built in the 12th century by a local Koli chief and later strengthened by the Siddis, or the Habshis, the East African pirates and sea-hardened sailors who arrived in India through the sea route. With its 19 bastions that survive to this day and its corroding cannons, the Janjira Fort has remained impregnable throughout history. All the efforts of the British, Dutch and Portuguese to defeat the Siddis were unsuccessful. Even Shivaji and his son, Sambhaji, who tried to capture the fort many times during their reigns failed in all their attempts.

Janjira remained an independent state with allegiance to the Mughals and the Marathas at different times of history, till 1947 when its occupants fled. Janjira Fort is now in ruins. Its 12 metre walls, made of granite and once considered insurmountable from all sides, remain so even to this day. But the walls are crumbling due to the sea and the weather. There is a single entry point through a gate that faces the Maharashtra coast on its eastern side. A much smaller rabbit-gate opens towards the Arabian Sea, built perhaps to escape by jumping off into the waiting boats in case the fort was captured. Not many know of this escape route because it was never used. The people who stayed in the fort were fierce warriors who didn't allow anyone to capture the fort. It is also rumoured that a tunnel exists which goes all the way under the sea up to the coast.

Inside the fort, there are two fresh water ponds for collecting rain water. When the fort was in use, besides these reservoirs, there were quarters for officers, an armoury, a mosque and a granary. At present the insides of the fort are in a state of disuse, due to the forest that has reclaimed it completely. Trees, thorny bushes, shrubs and creepers can be seen frolicking in merriment, edging one another for space. The foliage is so thick that visitors who now arrive using a ferry from the Murud jetty, a journey that takes them about half an hour, can't get past a few metres from the entrance. The remaining 300 metres of the fort remain impregnable even now, albeit due to Mother Nature and not the Siddi warriors.

The fort is controlled by the tourism department of the Government of Maharashtra and to ensure it stays that way, a police guard mans the main gate from nine in the morning till six in the evening. He takes the last ferry out of the fort and thereafter, it goes off the world's retina.

Without anyone's knowledge, the real activity began in the fort at night. Right under the water reservoir to the north there was a large secret chamber where people who had rested the whole day got up right after sunset and began their tutored work. The chamber was like a citadel and no light could escape outside it. A diesel generator provided the required power.

The evening Andy was shot in Mumbai, four men were talking in this chamber. Their heads were almost touching each other and their voices just a whisper. People whispered in a secure environment only when they were scared. Or when they knew dangers lurked near. Abdul, the leader of the four, was the one who spoke. The others just listened. He was their boss and they had faith in him.

Abdul had received a message that their location had been compromised. This meant that they had to be ready to leave the fort whenever ordered. There would be no time. Time though, was not the real worry. The real worry was that they had to remove all traces of what they were doing and take the equipment along with them. Once they were at a safe distance from the fort, the incriminating evidence had to be buried under the sea at a suitable distance and depth. This was the worrying part.

Right from the time he was entrusted with the job of making the dirty bomb with nuclear material in its core, Abdul knew problems could only arise if he was ever asked to remove his traces. He was aware that this was impossible, as nuclear traces took hundreds of years, sometimes thousands to wither away. He had prayed to God religiously, not to put him in such a dire situation. He knew all he needed was a secure place for about six months, the necessary ingredients and equipment, a good source of water, reliable power and the help of three or four men whom he could trust.

But it seemed that their luck had run out. One more week was still required to finish the bomb. It was a small bomb, just the size of a suitcase that could easily be carried to any place and detonated using a remote control device. Though the bomb was small, its effect wasn't. In a crowded Indian city it was capable of killing thousands and crippling another thousand for life. It was a potent weapon, and he had happily built it for use against the infidels. Abdul considered it his religious duty to teach the Indians a lesson. The very Indians who were friends with Israel, the very Indians who were the murderers of innocents in Kashmir.

He had no idea where the bomb was intended to be used and he didn't care less. He knew it would be used on Indian soil, and in India everyone was his enemy. His job was limited to making a bomb that would do maximum damage and he was pleased with the progress he had made. His helpers were young and stayed silent, listening to his big plans as if he were God. They were Pashtuns, known for their loyalty all over Pakistan — just like him.

It had been easy, like a dream. Till now.

Abdul had a contingency plan in his mind and he explained it now to his team. Each person was told exactly what was expected out of him and a practice run was performed at night. In the end, Abdul was satisfied. They had an inflated rubber dingy with two 100 horse power OBMs. Using the foot pump to fill it up, they pushed it back under the shrubs after covering it with a thick black rubber mat to save it from the thorns and shrubs. The escape plan was final. He stopped briefing them, looked at the brightly lit room and ushered them back to work. If the enemy was slow they might get more time. If he worked harder with his team, he hoped to reduce the balance one week by at least two days. There was still hope, and he would do his damned best.

13

onica reached home and shut herself in. The meeting with Krishna Bedi at his farm house had drained her completely. She was now almost certain that he would try to harm Andy. But what she couldn't get was why? Andy had just moments ago confirmed that he indeed was at Mumbai and KB knew that from before. This meant that KB's men were keeping a track of Andy.

Monica kept her purse aside and crashed on the sofa. Her breath was slightly laboured and her face was covered in sweat. She didn't feel the cold in the room as a cloud of uncertainty engulfed her. She had never thought she would have to live through such a situation. Ever since she started working for the magazine, she was never comfortable with KB's real intentions. But she wasn't scared. The world had never been fair to her. So she didn't care. She wasn't the least bit bothered what her boss was up to with his own money and his own game.

Monica wanted a job and this opportunity came her way when she needed it the most. Everyone had turned her away. She had got tired of borrowing money from her friends. They had started avoiding her calls. Many of them were demanding their money back. Her lovers had dried out. It was clear — she had reached a dead-end. She was 32 then, an 'old' model, whom no one in the world wanted to associate with. She felt pathetic, ugly and unwanted.

She accepted this job out of vengeance and her life changed. KB said he would pay her well and she could write whatever she wanted. She had complete independence, except the occasional stories she had to run the way KB wanted them. She knew it was unethical when she eventually published them. But what in this world wasn't? The world had been cruel to her and now she couldn't give a damn.

As long as KB lived, the magazine would survive. She hoped whatever plans he had would eventually work out in her overall interest, but there were still times when she was worried. He had been reasonable with her. He paid her well and it was only because of him that her social status had been restored. She had returned all the money borrowed from her friends and now lived a life of comfort. She was alive and happy.

The day Andy walked in for an interview she was

pleasantly surprised. He spoke of things that were opposite to her new beliefs. He talked about truth, loyalty and ethics. She always admired him. She also found him hard to resist. She decided to hire him. He looked different. Sending him to Tilakpur had been a tough decision for her. She had chosen her job over Andy. But it turned out to be a big mistake.

She wasn't interested at that time at what exactly was there at Tilakpur. Her only interest was a revelation which would help her pull the worm in the graph of popularity up again. When she saw Andy lying unconscious on the road, she was petrified. She had tried her best to explain to him that going back was dangerous. But he hadn't listened to her. Adding to her misery, Andy was now in Mumbai and working on a case she hadn't authorized.

She had to save Andy somehow. Monica reached for the phone and hesitated for a second. Then she dialled the number. The phone was off, but it must have been intentional. She knew Andy was keeping his phone off so that people couldn't track him down. She decided to wait for him to call.

Monica felt the urge to go to Mumbai and be with Andy in these strange times. It wasn't practical though. With no other option, Monica decided to wait for the phone to ring, hoping that Andy would call. She felt miserable.

The Police Commissioner of Mumbai was a tall man. He had been working for the past thirty years and was known for his conviction, fairness and astute sense of the present. When a journalist called Andy arrived at his office, he was somewhat surprised. He observed him through the glass wall sitting in the chair, calm and composed. When people came to the Commissioner, even if they hadn't committed any crime, the mere fact that they were meeting the head of the police made them fidgety. But not this man. He sat, his feet crossed at his ankles, breathing normally and looking at him straight through the glass. Only Andy Karan saw his own reflection in it.

When the man said his name was Andy and that he was working with Intelligence, he was no longer surprised. Now he knew this man obviously fancied working for Intelligence and was just leading him up the gum tree. The man could be working alone and was probably mentally challenged too. Yet he reconsidered his thoughts. As a policeman he had learnt it the hard way that first impressions were more often than not, wrong. He knew the rapists, those who committed the most heinous of all known crimes, were the most innocent looking, and the real gangsters resembled senile old age home inhabitants. Appearances and motivations of people were both deceptive.

He concluded that Andy Karan was certainly someone working alone. The man said that he was from Delhi. But there was no memo from the Home Ministry or the Delhi Police about this meeting. If this man was indeed working on a top secret mission, the Police Commissioner would have been informed. It was simple protocol. He heard Andy out of practice and sent him away as soon as it looked decent.

After he was gone, the Police Commissioner asked one of his men to follow him and find out more about him. He wouldn't let the stranger vanish just like that. Reception had intimated that he carried a pistol too. Therefore, if not to verify whether he really worked for Intelligence or not, he had to make sure that no damage was done to the peace and property of Mumbai.

The Police Commissioner was going through a few urgent files on his table when the phone rang — the line reserved only for emergencies. He quickly grabbed the receiver and sat up alert. 'Go.'

The voice on the other end said Andy had been shot by a long range rifle. He was informed of the location.

The Commissioner quickly assessed the situation and ordered, 'Take him to Bombay Hospital.' Bombay Hospital was only a kilometre away.

He hung up and called the surgeon who dealt with bullet injury cases and who also headed the hospital. After he was done, he sat in silence wondering who this man really was. The man had said he needed back-up at Murud Janjira. What was brewing there? As far as he knew, the fort was abandoned with no traces of life. The island was dark at night and during the day, there were tourists all around. Half a kilometre of sea separated the island from the mainland. What possible use could anyone have for a place like that which wasn't even connected by land?

He reached for the phone and called the Home Ministry in Delhi. It was time and he had an illusory feeling that there was something just out of sight. He got the required information and rushed to the hospital. He was determined to save the man's life. Perhaps he could.

Krishna Bedi was worried. The plan that initially looked fool proof was beginning to fray along the edges. He knew if he didn't act fast, the entire operation would be lost. There would be consequences too. Besides losing his money, he would end up behind bars. 'Stop it! You know you are exaggerating. Don't let it get to you!' He smiled forcefully, looking in the mirror. No one could ever put a man like Krishna Bedi in jail. There was no such jail anywhere in the world that could contain him. He had money and therefore, unlimited power. Greedy politicians could be bought easily. He had several of them in his pocket already.

KB's bomb would only be used as a last resort. Not because he had sympathy for the people who would be killed, but merely because he could achieve his desired results by using it as a warning. But now the location where the bomb was being made had been compromised. If the people working there were caught red-handed, they would point their fingers at Kismet Khan. Through Kismet, the government would eventually wind up to him, though the chances were still slightly remote. But he wasn't prepared to leave the option open.

Krishna Bedi once again thought what a dirty bomb could do if detonated successfully. One, it would create unprecedented panic among the people as they got contaminated. Not many would be killed, he knew, as there would be no shock and heat wave as in a nuclear fission explosion. Yet, thousands would die and it was enough to make people run amok in panic. And two, the nation's economy would be affected irreversibly. Investors would pack their bags and run away. Foreign investment projects would be abandoned. And then the cost of the clean-up. This would paralyze the government. In the contaminated areas they would be required to tear down buildings, get rid of the top soil, empty water sources, move thousands of people and erect temporary accommodation for them. Though detonating the bomb was not in the original plan, he somehow wanted to go ahead and do it now.

The phone rang. The messages brought his natural smile back. He sank lower in his chair. Both Kapoor and Andy had been killed by his men. The situation was normalizing, but he was worried if any of these two men had passed the information about Murud Janjira on to someone else. Just like Tilakpur, now was the time to escape from the fort. But before he could call Kismet Khan and share his plan, he wanted to give this news to Monica.

He wanted to relish the sadistic pleasure himself by giving the news first as he knew that Monica thought of Andy as a romantic companion. She had done enough damage, even if he knew it was without her knowledge.

As he waited for Monica to answer the phone, he wondered if it was time to kill her too. He somehow liked her — not in the way a man likes a woman, but as a fellow human being. There was a naivety in Monica which he found fascinating. She was doing a good job for him, keeping his magazine popular. If he killed her he would have to look for her replacement and train a new person to do her job. He decided against killing Monica just as she came on line — at least for the time being.

'Monica, I'm calling to inform you that our reporter Andy is dead.' He paused, the receiver of the phone pressed hard against his ear to hear her exact reaction, and then added, equally firmly, 'And so is the old man he was working for.'

There was silence on the other end and then he heard the phone drop with a sound, and he hung up. A thin smile broke wide against his lips. Nothing had changed. They were on track. Except that now he wanted to execute his Plan B.

Bombay Hospital is located on Marine Lines. With five lakh square feet of covered area, it has almost a 1,000 beds

and more than 200 doctors, besides the numerous special-
ists available on call. The hospital comprises four buildings
and has a reputation to match the best hospitals in India
and the world in terms of infrastructure and expertise.

The Police Commissioner headed straight for the operation theatre on the fourth floor. Of the 20 odd operation theatres in the hospital, he knew this was where
patients with bullet injuries were brought. He found his
man at the gate of the theatre. Neither smiled, though
their eyes shone for a fraction of a second in greeting.

'He will survive, thanks to the bullet proof jacket. But
he's lost a lot of blood.'

The Police Commissioner stared hard at the glass
doors of the operation theatre where it was written in
red, as if in blood, NO ENTRY, EXCEPT ON MEDICAL
DUTY.

'Gun?' he asked.

'.50 Barrett. M 82.'

The Commissioner drew in his breath. The M 82 was
the close cousin of the M 107 that the commandos of
the Mumbai police used. No human in the world could
survive that kind of a weapon. He was surprised. The
M 82 was an expensive, American-make weapon and he
was hearing of its use for the first time in India. It meant
there was an enemy out there who was smarter and better equipped with the latest ammunition and technology,

no doubt. This wasn't a conventional fight. His worries intensified.

He made a brief call and alerted someone to find out about the arrival of this weapon in India, more importantly in Mumbai.

Then he turned to the man, 'How much more time?'

'The doctor said one hour. They are stitching the wound. The bullet pierced the body armour, but lost its tenacity. It's lodged in a muscle on his chest.'

'Source of armour?'

'Indian Army.'

The Commissioner recalled his meeting. He knew this man was different, but only now did he learn that he was from the Army. Was he here on Army duty? Since when had the government started sending in armed forces without consultation? He felt disgusted.

The glass doors swung open and a doctor came out. He greeted the Commissioner and smiled as if in relief.

'Lucky guy. The body armour saved him. The bullet was lodged superficially and we have removed it.'

'Thanks, doc. This is a top secret issue. So we expect total silence on this. Can I see the bullet?'

The doctor smiled, shoved his hands into his apron and pulled out a small plastic container with the bullet.

It looked menacing because of its shine and sheer size. The Commissioner emptied the bullet into his hand and moved it up and down to feel its weight before returning it.

'I'd like to take my patient to a safe house. Is he conscious?'

'Yes, and free to move. You can take him walking if you like.' There was a hint of sarcasm in his voice.

The doctor returned to the operation theatre and the Commissioner winked to his assistant. The man went his way. He had to check if the route was clear. The doctor had said the ambulance was waiting at the rear exit. But the Commissioner had other plans.

14

ndy was wheeled out of the operation theatre shortly afterwards. The Police Commissioner and a man he did not recognize were waiting to greet him right outside. The Commissioner smiled and Andy thanked him for saving his life by bringing him to the hospital in time. The other man looked at him without any expression.

Andy had no idea what to expect next. At the moment he was in the custody of the police. The doctor had already told him that the bullet proof jacket had saved his life. Andy had brought the jacket with him from Delhi, where he had convinced a friend from his Army days to hand him an old, used jacket. He smiled at his presence of his mind. Brief preparations go a long way, his training instructor at the Academy used to insist. Like always, falling back on solid training methods had saved his life.

Till Andy was shot, he was sure that in a busy market like Colaba, no one would use a weapon like a pistol or a rifle. But he was proved wrong once again. He expected to see someone come up and attack him with a knife. He remembered the large man he had neutralized at the phone booth minutes before he was shot. That was their method. The drunkard at Tilakpur was also killed by a knife a year ago. This was new. Either they were getting desperate or they had more professionals now on Andy's back. He had no way of knowing that the same weapon was used at Tilakpur too, the morning after Ram Avtar's death to kill an unknown person in the mustard fields. But as the killers had buried the dead, no one came to know about the weapon that was used for the killing.

Now he was being wheeled out of the hospital. The Commissioner walked on his left. The three of them entered the lift and the two men stood on both his sides. Neither talked. They seemed to be sure of where they were going.

The lift door opened on the ground floor. It was noisy and people stared at a patient being wheeled out. Visitors always stared at the patients in hospitals, Andy had noticed. Perhaps it was a sinister way of realizing that they were safer and healthier. Others were sick and they weren't. It was a relief, something that dwarfed the other worries that people always had. He resisted the urge to smile, looking at people who behaved exactly as he had expected.

The wheel chair wobbled on the tar road outside for a while. They reached a black car. Andy had expected an ambulance, but this was an Ambassador. It looked exactly like a government vehicle and he felt relieved. He was with the right people. The Commissioner said a few words of assurance and asked if he could get up. He did, felt a flash of pain travel through his shoulder, but managed to get into the car in the end. The Commissioner got into the back seat next to him, as the other man hurried to the front. The driver was already inside. He turned and gave Andy a sheepish smile. On his forehead, he wore a vermillion *tilak* and a Gandhi *topi* covered his salt and pepper hair, tufts of which peeped out from the sides.

The black car rolled off with four of them inside. The windows had tinted glasses and additional white curtains that enhanced their privacy. No one spoke. After ten minutes the car rolled on to a deserted road and turned into what looked like an apartment block complex to Andy. He got down and felt the same flash again. Two buildings rose in the evening sky side by side. Their car had stopped right in the middle.

There was another man waiting between the two buildings, who brought a wobbling wheel chair to a halt near him. Andy collapsed in it, playing his cards by the book. As the wheel chair started to move, he noticed that the man who had travelled with them from the hospital stayed back with the driver. His place was now taken by the man who had brought the wheel chair. The two resembled each other so much that if he had seen them separately he wouldn't have been able to make out one from the other.

The lift door closed on them and reopened on the twentieth floor. He was wheeled into a flat and the man who brought him in, backed away after he lay down on the bed in one of the bedrooms.

There was pin drop silence. He was so way up from the road below that he couldn't even hear the vehicles any more. In any case, there weren't many of them on this road, he had noticed while coming in. Perhaps it ended in a blind on one side.

'You're in a safe house, Andy. This belongs to the police department.' The Commissioner explained to Andy after he had comfortably settled in the bed.

'Thank you.'

'The person who brought you in will be with you 24x7. He will sleep in the other room. He has weapons and is trained. There will be a cook for homemade food, which he will supervise personally. Your job is to just stay here. Rest, eat well and recover soon. Okay?'

Andy nodded. He was thinking. His life had been saved, yet he was dreading the prospect of being locked up in a safe house for many days. He thought of Monica.

'I wouldn't have troubled you by asking questions at this moment, but as you can see, we are in a very precarious situation. Do you think you can talk for a few minutes?'

Andy told him everything. All facts. Nothing was hidden. He had no choice. The man was really the Police Commissioner and he had met him at his office this very morning. In any case, old man Kapoor was missing and he had no one to turn to. He told him about Monica, Dewanchand, and Kapoor, the people at Tilakpur including Gulabo, and the big-angry man, and finally, Hakim. It took him more than two hours. In the meantime, Mumbai was covered in darkness. He finished and whispered that he was feeling tired. The Commissioner smiled.

'Let me see what best I can do. I'll get Murud Janjira checked. I don't think there is any scope for explosives to be stored there...the place is infested with snakes and centipedes with vegetation so thick that even water percolates to the ground with difficulty. But nevertheless, I'll send a search party by boat and get it rummaged.'

'All right.'

Now more deliberately, as if he was thinking while speaking, the Commissioner continued, 'I also feel that since Murud Janjira's name has come up in your investigations, it is more likely that something is brewing at Murud village itself. I should get its surroundings checked. I'll ask my boys to camp there for a few days. As for the Prime Minister's visit tomorrow, I have already called in more troops from Pune.'

Andy smiled. The Commissioner walked away. As if on cue, the other man walked in immediately — like he had been waiting outside all this while.

'My name is Lokhande. If you need anything just press that.' He pointed to a push switch next to Andy's bed and disappeared.

Now was the time to think. This was Andy's last thought. The drugs that had been administered into his body dragged him into a cocoon of inky nothing and he slept it off.

Monica got up with a start. Her head ached. She was still on the sofa and the phone was at her feet. Then she woke up to reality. Andy had died. She felt incredibly low and lonely. Life suddenly seemed empty, a useless waste of time. Her boss was responsible, she was sure after the call. She began hating him so much that she wanted to go to his farm right now, get a gun and kill the bastard.

Monica staggered to the balcony of her flat. She looked down three floors to the concrete. It was dark outside. She had no idea what time it was. It could be early in the evening, or maybe just before dawn, or midnight. Anything. Time didn't matter. There were no people down, she noticed. So she just figured it was after midnight.

She climbed on the railing, both her arms extended to her sides for balance. She felt death and it didn't scare her. For the first time in her life, the prospect of dying didn't make her uncomfortable. She brought her hands down slowly, losing her balance bit by bit in the process, feeling her body sway in the cold breeze. Then halfway, she stopped.

Monica stood like that on the railing of her balcony for five minutes, her numb mind wondering what she would do. She had no idea of her intentions. She wondered if she was high enough to fall and die. What if she didn't? Surely the fall would cripple her for life. That would be worse. Her friends would visit and say they were sorry without even meaning it. She would have no job and no money and one day she would die in her own house without anyone knowing about it. And after several days, someone would notice the stink from her flat. They would break open the door and watch in horror, their noses covered with handkerchiefs at the maggots falling from her body. Monica shuddered.

Her options were clear. Either she lives, or she dies. If she lives, she had to set the equation right. Her anger rose. Krishna Bedi had to pay for killing Andy. This was more perfect, because if she failed, they would kill her. But if she turned the tables on them, she would take over the magazine and run it like nothing ever happened. Run it by the rules, ethics, just as Andy would have wanted to. She would try and forget Andy, and having her revenge would make it even easier.

Monica got down from the railing. She was not giving up without a fight. The decision had been made.

Andy woke up late. The bright daylight made him squint his eyes and through a blurred vision he saw the Commissioner seated in front of him. There was another person with him who seemed vaguely familiar. Andy wondered who he was. Till the stethoscope gave him away. He was the doctor who had operated upon him.

The doctor came close and said, 'You're doing well. Nothing to worry. The wound has begun to heal and it shouldn't take more than a week.'

A week? Andy's heart sank. Like the Karan of Mahabharata, his future was forever grim, no matter how righteous he remained. His honesty, uprightness and sacrifices weren't enough to make him the winner. He remembered his mother and wondered how she would feel if she saw him right now. He knew she would curse herself for his failures. But Andy was determined to win. Just like Karan, despite all odds, he had faith.

The doctor gave him an injection and said he had to leave for the hospital. He had a new emergency to deal with. After he was gone, the Commissioner moved forward and whispered, 'Don't read the newspapers today.'

Andy frowned.

'Because according to the headlines, you're dead.'

Andy's face retained its frown, but after two seconds it spread in a smile.

'Good one, Sir.'

'The doctor said one week, but I think you'll be fine in three days. I have a plan and I hope you will cooperate.'

Andy waited for more.

'Don't shave. We will give you a wig, a set of dentures to be put in your mouth to change the jaw line...the stubble will add a shabby look. I'll also get you a pair of shoes with different heels sizes. It'll make you limp. There will be a man who will work on your eyebrows. Even your girlfriend won't recognize you after that.'

'I don't have a girlfriend.' Andy kicked himself silently for replying to a comment that was just used to prove a point.

The Commissioner thankfully, ignored Andy's response and walked away, patting him lightly on his cheek. Almost like a father.

Lokhande brought a cup of freshly made milk tea. Andy took a sip and it felt like heaven. Simple pleasures of life make living worthwhile. The man asked what he wanted to eat for breakfast. Recalling the Commissioner's three days period, he asked for eggs, ham, bread, milk and orange juice. And bananas. He needed his strength back fast. The man said he hadn't heard of ham in his life, but he could arrange for some chicken *pakoras*. Andy smiled cheerily at him. They would do.

By the time he finished his breakfast, it was almost mid-day. He thought of Monica and realized the error at that moment. By agreeing with the Commissioner he had closed the doors on Monica. Now he wouldn't be able to tell her that he was alive. It was too dangerous to call her up. Her phone in all probabilities, was tapped. He felt miserable. But since every problem had a way out, he realized he could find a solution here as well. It took him five minutes.

The doctor had sent a male nurse to change the dressing. Lokhande brought him in. Andy eyed him with suspicion, but the man just looked at him blankly.

He got down from the bed with the help of the man and inspected the wound in the bathroom mirror after the bandage was removed. Every time he moved his upper body, a flash of pain shot through it; but its intensity had dulled by now. The nurse changed his dressing and gave him a shot. Then he smiled and went away.

Lokhande returned after escorting the nurse out and asked what Andy wanted for lunch.

'Maharashtrian *thali*.'

Lokhande beamed and retracted out of his room in a hurry. He got busy with the cook in the kitchen as Andy got back to his thinking.

He pushed the button after ten minutes.

'Lokhande, I want my room at the Trident to be vacated and my bag brought here.' He gave him the room number.

15

The familiarity of his bag brought a smile on Andy's face. He thanked Lokhande for bringing it to him so fast and took out his laptop. Before switching it on, he paused for a while. What if his enemies were still monitoring the internet connection he used? Each connection has a unique IP address and it can be as easily tracked as a mobile phone. If he used it now, his position and the mail he sends to Monica might also be read. He yanked out the internet dongle and kept it away from his laptop.

He asked Lokhande if there was a way he could have a virgin dongle. The man disappeared without a word and was back after an hour.

'Use this one.' He thrust a new dongle towards him, which he must have got through his police contacts. This meant that the police would certainly monitor his internet activity now. It was good that he had nothing to hide from them.

But there was another problem. What if the enemy was monitoring Monica's ID? He thought of sending an e-mail to one of his friends in Delhi, the Army friend he borrowed the bullet proof jacket from. He could go to Monica's house and deliver the message personally. But even this option had a hitch. What if they were keeping a watch on Monica? However, now with him out of the way and probably Mr Kapoor too, Andy imagined the enemy wouldn't be wasting resources checking people out randomly. They would be using them instead to execute their plan. Yet he couldn't decide if asking his friend was the right thing to do. He turned to Lokhande to find out more about the dongle and was relieved to discover that it was registered under a fake name and address that was more than ten kilometres away from the safe house.

Andy scrubbed himself with a warm, moist towel in the bathroom, careful not to wet the bandage and changed into clean clothes from his bag. He felt fresh and his skin breathed in relief. Lokhande took away the used clothes. When Andy was sipping his tea, he got an idea. Monica and Andy had shared many moments with each other, chit-chatted about unimportant things as colleagues in the same office. He hoped to remind her of one of their unique discussions. Monica was sharp and he knew if he used the message well, she would understand in no time.

He remembered the time when they had kissed at the office a few days ago and were on the verge of literally doing it. Till some idiot knocked on the door. He smiled recalling those moments. The memory left him aroused. And surprised. Perhaps his mind and instincts were not in sync and sometimes it was better to follow one's instincts. He knew he had to come clean for her. She was as lonely as him and she cared about him.

Monica had confessed that two of her lovers had used and ditched her. Perhaps this was something he could use in his message. Andy opened a new e-mail account and called it thethirdlover@gmail.com. He knew Monica's ID by heart as he had used it often to mail her his stories for the magazine.

He sent her a simple message.

'You can't be third time unlucky. But for that you have to stop believing.'

Andy hit 'Send' and hoped that if someone was indeed monitoring her inbox, he wouldn't make much out of it. He asked her not to believe. People believed what they read, saw or heard. He wanted her to understand that he wasn't dead and no matter how she received this message — read, saw or heard — she shouldn't believe it. The 'thirdlover' ID was also expected to give her a clue about the sender.

Andy now waited patiently, eating a banana. After about forty minutes, he got a reply. It was from a new ID too.

'Can you guess what I am doing at this moment?'

It was Monica, and smartly she had also created a new email ID. It had taken her more than half an hour to reply. This naturally meant that she had created this new email ID using another computer terminal. Smart. But was she at home or at an internet café? In any case, it did not matter.

Chewing the end of a pencil. He typed and then added another sentence.

'After two days, wait at the best resort in Murud village for Atul Rastogi.'

He sent off the message and sat waiting, his fingers drumming the side table. The reply arrived in seconds.

'I am Ramya. It was nice meeting you.'

Andy logged out. Calling Monica to Murud was bringing her closer to the danger, no doubt, but he badly wanted to meet her. Before taking the biggest risk of his life, he wanted to see her at least once. In any case, Monica would stay back at the motel when he went to the island fortress with police help. He knew she would at least be safe.

Abdul and his team were now working fifteen hours a day. As soon as the last ferry with the police guard departed in the evening at six, he and his team would start working and they continued till minutes before the ferry arrived back at nine the next morning. Even meal breaks were reduced from one hour to fifteen minutes.

Though they worked fast, they were taking all precautions and going by the book. They couldn't risk an accident. An accident would mean death for them. Not that anyone of them feared death, but the entire operation would fail. And Abdul didn't like failures. More than twenty-four hours had elapsed, but the orders to escape had yet not come. This was good news for him and it added to the confidence of the team.

He stopped them briefly and said, 'We need three more days now.' He was smiling, like he could sense the victory. The others smiled in equal measure.

During the night while they worked, for the first time, he had asked one of his men to be outside to guard them against any visitors. This had become necessary after the warning. The man on guard duty was properly briefed and armed with a pistol and a long range rifle. The others worked even harder to compensate for his absence. Better safe than sorry.

Monica was ecstatic. She knew it was Andy Karan she was communicating with. Not only had he conveyed that he was alive, he had also revealed what he thought of himself — her third lover. The third lover who was also the best one of the lot.

Andy had asked her to meet him at Murud. She had never heard of the name. Seated in the cyber café about hundred metres from her flat, she checked where it was then gasped in surprise. What on earth could Andy be doing at Murud, staying at a resort there? It seemed like the unlikeliest of places someone would go visiting!

Also, why did he contact her after two days and not immediately? But she didn't give it much thought then. For her he was alive and willing to be her lover. That was all she needed to know. She began to dream of a home with Andy. Children too. It made her life seem complete and suddenly the world around her was so much brighter. But could she have children since she was nearly forty? Perhaps she could. She decided to consult a doctor.

She got back to her flat and was humming an old Hindi film song, when her phone rang. She stiffened and took the call. It was KB.

'How are you?'

She said she was fine.

'I hope you're not hiding something from me?'

This came as a shot from the blue. KB had never asked her this question. She knew that he had complete faith in her. Then what had changed suddenly?

'Sir, why would I hide anything from you?' she put the question back to her boss.

'Good, good...But remember, if you do ever lie to me, be warned that there would be no reprieve.' The threat was clear in his voice and Monica froze.

It was a bit too farfetched, but she considered her visit to the café. Did one of KB's men see her going there? That would certainly raise suspicions, as someone like her who had internet on her computer and her iPad wouldn't need to visit an internet café. She should have thought of that. Was it therefore possible that someone was watching her movements and reporting to KB?

She didn't like the silence on the phone. It was making the warning echo endlessly.

'Sir, I would never lie to you. I have no reason. You are my boss and you pay me money. I have always been loyal to you.'

'Stay loyal.' Then the line went dead.

Monica's mouth remained open for a while as she considered the threat. There surely was something amiss. KB had never treated her so shoddily. And it could be nothing other than her visit to the internet café. She decided to find out. As a media person, she had some idea how to work things out.

An hour later she stepped out of her house without making any sound. The corridor was quiet. It was late evening and the cold outside made the hair at the back of her neck stand. Or was it due to the adventure she was suddenly in the midst of? Instead of taking the lift, she took the stairs and reached the seventh floor. The seventh floor of her apartment had a connecting corridor with the building adjacent to it. She crossed over to the other building and came down by the lift.

When she reached the other side of her building, she looked around her. Monica, her head covered in a scarf and her jacket collar turned up, looked different. From here, she had a clear view of her building's entrance. She could see three men and began observing them closely. One smoked a cigarette, the second was speaking to someone on a mobile phone and the third was kicking dirt on the road. Any one of them could have been KB's men. Or they could just be young men biding their time.

But she wasn't interested in knowing which one of them was KB's man. She wanted to know if they followed her to the internet café and checked the computer she had used.

Leaving the men right there she walked briskly to the café and went inside. The person at the table, who maintained a log of the users and handled the money, was a young boy who sported a goatee. He looked malnourished when he smiled half-heartedly at Monica.

'Yes, Aunty?'

Though he was barely seventeen or eighteen, Monica didn't like him calling her an 'aunty'.

'I am not your Aunty. I could be your girlfriend.' She winked and the young boy was embarrassed.

'Sorry. You were here sometime back too. Can I help you?'

'When I finished my work and went away, did someone come and use the same computer I was on?'

'Yes, there was a man. He said he wanted to use the internet and I asked him to use table number 2. But he insisted on using the same computer you had used.'

'And?'

'And...I allowed him.'

'Is there a way you can check what he did while he was here?'

"Yes...give me a second.' The young boy swung in his chair and began his work on the main server on his side. He looked back in a minute.

'He didn't do anything except open the files you had used.'

'I had sent a mail. Do you think he could have read the contents of my mail?'

'No, no way... that would be impossible to do in such a short time.'

Monica winked at him. He showed her a name the man had scrawled in the register and a copy of his ID. She paid no attention as she knew both were fake. Monica bent down, turned her bright red lips into a pout and kissed the air before the young man's face. Then she walked away, leaving the poor kid to deal with the effect she had caused.

She used the same way back, reached her flat and locked herself in. So this was it. KB was watching her. Maybe because he expected her to react after Andy's death. He was hoping treason from her and that is what he would get, she thought angrily. He now knew that she had chosen to send a mail from an internet café and not used her own network from home. But he didn't know that Andy was alive and he also didn't know where she was headed. She smiled.

And then it hit her. She had used Google Maps to figure out where Murud was. She kicked herself. The man must have seen that. It meant part of her intentions was compromised. She had shown interest in Murud and since Andy had asked her to come there, there must be something big waiting to happen. Something in which her boss had a stake. But they still didn't know that Andy was alive. She decided to take a chance.

KB sank back in his chair with a wry smile on his lips. Andy and Mr Kapoor had both been killed. While Andy was shot by a rifle, Mr Kapoor was run over by a bus when he was going to Lodhi Gardens for his morning walk.

Even the man, Hakim, who they suspected to be working for the intelligence was dead.

Kismet Khan's last message had been very encouraging. The bomb would be ready in two days. He had not agreed with KB's 'plan B' to evacuate his men from the island. KB saw his point. Evacuating now meant throwing the bomb into the sea as it was too unstable to be transported in its present state. The disturbance might cause it to detonate and all their efforts would be in vain.

KB had already made plans for the bomb to be brought to Tilakpur. This was where he would keep the bomb. 'The Dirty Bomb for Dirty Politics'. He knew the bomb was very volatile owing to the nuclear material inside its core, so he had to transport it with utmost care. Initially, he had planned to bring it by road from Murud to Delhi. But now he was thinking of alternate routes too.

While the bomb waited at Tilakpur, his plan was to negotiate with the government and if they didn't agree, he would tell them to face the consequences. Once he gave his warning, he knew how it would play out. He would be arrested, all his accounts frozen and his house and office rummaged. But he had nothing to fear. Anticipating these moves, he had already taken all the necessary precautions. Governments were always so predictable. They went by the book and KB had spent time reading the book. That was his real investment. One of the many reasons that made him such a successful businessman.

He was confused when he received new information about Monica. His hunch had been right. Monica was no longer the Monica he knew. Ever since she had started liking Andy, things had turned different. But what did she know? She had sent a mail to someone and she chose to send it from a café instead of her house. He knew her email IDs and his people couldn't find anything amiss there. Did she have a secret account?

He was also told she looked up Murud town on the map. There was no business for her to look for such an obscure place. There was nothing newsworthy happening there. This wasn't an innocent journalistic thing. She definitely knew more. Who was her collaborator? He came to dead ends every time. According to his information, only Kapoor and Andy knew about Murud. Both were dead now. But Monica also knew, and only just recently. Who told her this? His instincts told him it was time. They needed to shift the bomb. If they took precautions, they could put it in a boat and take it to mainland. But he knew Kismet Khan wouldn't agree. He felt he should have chosen a better partner in this whole mess.

He couldn't help it. He had to warn Kismet Khan. He reached for the phone and dialled a number.

'Two have been wiped out, but one more knows about it. Possibility of even more knowing. I think we should hurry now. We need a forward post at Murud to buy time if they come charging.'

The voice on the other side groaned and agreed. He hung up. Now all he could do was wait.

16

For the past two days Andy had been resting — eating, sleeping or reading paperbacks. He finished one of the latest thrillers, enjoying it immensely. Occasionally, he'd check the newspapers too. Though Lokhande was doing all he could, Andy was trapped in a boring world. As a man of action, his nerves weren't accustomed to so much peace. At the same time, he also knew this was an inescapable situation.

He remembered the call from the Police Commissioner. 'My people have found nothing amiss at the Janjira Fort or at Murud village.'

'Yet,' he added immediately. 'I have ordered them to camp at Murud for some more time and maintain vigil.'

There was a pause and then he said, as if on an afterthought, 'The man you mentioned, Hakim, the IB informer... we've found him. It seems he was killed on the same day he met you.'

This was a jolt to Andy. So the fear he saw in the man's eyes had been realized. He had seen his own death and therefore appeared completely shaken.

He was still thinking about Hakim when the doctor arrived. It was ten in the morning. The doctor removed the stitches and complimented him for healing faster than he had hoped. Andy smiled in return. It was a smile of reassurance he was giving to no one in particular. He was getting ready for action. Just like Karan of the Mahabharata, three attempts had been made on his life and he had survived them all. There would be more, surely. But unlike his mythological namesake, he didn't intend to die young.

Finally, it was the day he could leave the safe house. Andy had a proper bath after three days and he felt alive. The Commissioner had said that they would be watching his movements. He was in his vest and boxer shorts waiting for the much awaited job of his makeover.

The man who finally arrived to work on Andy was straight out of Bollywood. He had slender arms and moved, rather fluttered about as if he was not happy with the world, forever fussing and complaining.

The man said his name was Daniel, but he stressed so hard on the last syllable that it sounded like Daniela. After the introductions were made and having shaken a limp hand, Andy asked him if he had a boyfriend and saw him smile shyly. Andy exchanged a few more pleasantries, as Daniel(a) got busy.

The dentures did change his jaw line. The stubble that had imprinted half his face readjusted in shape as the dentures were pushed in and Andy smiled. The same person he was used to seeing in the mirror looked different. But on careful observation, he realized that a few similarities remained. He wore the wig and watched bemused as two flicks of black hair fell on his forehead. Andy was used to combing his hair back and keeping his wide forehead clear of the hairy mess. His head that was covered in dark brown and wavy hair was now all black and straight. The similarities with the man in the mirror reduced further.

Daniel brought his face closer to Andy's till he was merely inches away and Andy waited, his breath halted, wondering what he was up to. The man reached for his eyebrows and started to pluck out odd hairs to alter their shape. Andy felt the stinging pain increase in intensity, but stayed still and quiet. After a few minutes, Daniel moved away. Andy caught himself in the mirror. All the similarities were gonenow. All that remained of Andy Karan was the colour of his skin and the proportion of his body.

The make-up guy had brought clothes too. Andy got

into trousers that flared at the bottom. As he wore his shoes he realized that the trousers mopped around the floor. The shirt was simple, with big brown and yellow checks. Andy saw himself in the mirror and was almost convinced that the man staring at him was indeed someone else. He walked and his left foot fell awkwardly, making him limp. The disguise was complete. He wasn't Andy Karan now. He needed a new name.

'My partner's name is Jagtap Chougale. Use that if you want...'

Andy shot a surprised smile at Daniel. He seemed to read Andy's thoughts. And perhaps he was already comparing Andy to his partner. It was time to send him back to Bollywood. Andy thanked him and winked at Lokhande, who held Daniel's shoulder and ushered him away even as he resisted slightly. Before he vanished from the view, he blew a kiss to Andy. Andy couldn't help but laugh. Apparently, he was quite the catch.

When he got back to the mirror and faced the new man in it, he was no longer smiling. His mind was busy. The last three days had helped him build a plan. He collected his bag, thanked Lokhande and walked out of the flat. There was no pain now and he was a new man. The enemy was convinced that he had been killed, so it was easier for him to catch them off guard.

Andy took a taxi from under the building and asked

him to be taken to VT station. He now had a new SIM card. The time was twelve in the afternoon. He was booked to stay at the Golden Duck Beach Resort at Murud under a false name. The name he had told Monica. The place was close to the jetty and he could meet her in the privacy of the resort. The Police Commissioner had provided him with a fake driving license too, which he could use at the reception for identification.

He ate a quick lunch at an Udipi restaurant near VT station and hired a private taxi to head towards Murud. Slowly, the megacity faded away in the background. Coconut trees and thatched roofed villages began appearing and disappearing on both the sides of the road. He drifted in and out of sleep. At four, he asked the driver to stop at a wayside restaurant for a tea break. The driver pulled over and informed Andy that it would take them another forty-five minutes or so to reach Murud.

Sipping tea, Andy replayed the plan in his head. The Commissioner had said there was nothing at the Janjira Fort. He recalled Hakim being certain about the fort having explosives. Maybe the police didn't check properly. When one works for the police and everything is required to be checked as per procedure, he may take it casually and adopt shortcuts without intending. It was an occupational hazard. Like in the Army, he recalled, some of his officer friends took the militants lightly. Until someone lost his life.

Being vigilant 24x7x365 was not possible and no amount of training could change it. So if the police took it lightly, they could easily have faltered. After meeting Monica and securing her at a safe place, he wanted to reach Janjira Fort early in the morning. An hour before sunrise. But for that he needed a boat. Now, this was the difficult part. If indeed there was someone at the fort, they would have people watching the fishing harbour. He would have to be discreet. But he knew it wasn't impossible.

There had to be a way. They were on the road again and as their taxi neared Murud he saw boats in the creeks the taxi crossed every few kilometres. His enemies would be watching the main fishing harbour and the Murud jetty. But what if he took a longer route? It excited him.

People protect their interests in islands by a simple, two fold strategy. From land, they concentrate on the island closest to it, and from the island, they monitor the boats approaching from the direction of the harbour. If Andy had to succeed, he had to surprise them on both these counts. A plan began to spawn in his mind as they negotiated an ugly, potholed stretch of road. Andy was at ease instead of showing disgust. With a little bit of luck, everything would perhaps work out for the best.

The driver was by now using the choicest of abuses. He said the Government didn't do anything to keep the roads in good condition. Andy remained quiet as the driver continued blaming the corrupt politicians adding that all the contractors were their bothers-in-law. He was really angry. Andy let him be and didn't react to his provocations. He wanted that man to have no memories of him when he got down.

He saw a milestone which said Murud was twenty kilometres away. Now was the time. After a few minutes, he asked the driver to slow down as he saw a creek approaching. The driver turned back to look at him, surprised. Andy repeated his instructions and the man threw his shoulders, murmured something in Marathi and stopped.

Andy walked to the bridge and looked down. The creek had three boats pulled to the sides. Nylon ropes peeped out from them and he traced their ends in anchors that were embedded in clay, fifty feet or so from the boats. He looked beyond and saw a few thatched roofs in the distance, smoke emanating through their tops.

He heard the driver approach him from behind.

'Sahib, what do you want? Please ask me. I'm a local person, I can help you.'

'Nothing. Can you take a picture of me with the creek in the background?' Andy handed him his phone.

The man looked around dumbfounded, unable to understand what his customer found worthy enough to photograph, but as someone who had been ferrying tourists in and around Mumbai for years now, he knew tourists were people with the weirdest choices. And even after ten years, it was impossible for him to gauge their requirements. He grumbled and clicked a picture.

They were on their way again. Murud was hardly even a decent civilization. It sprung up, a cluster of houses and then the taxi slowed down.

'Do you know the Golden Duck Beach Resort here?' Andy asked the driver.

The driver didn't reply but continued driving. He suddenly swerved right, entered an unmanned gate that was open and stopped. They were in front of a small room, the roof of which sloped, Manglorean tiles on the top. The season's rain had rendered some of the tiles black, amidst which new red ones shone in the late evening light. Andy got down and had a better view. The room had yellow walls and a man walked out towards them.

The driver handed him Andy's bag and stood waiting, scratching his chin. He seemed to be in a hurry. Andy paid him and walked into the small room. While he was signing his false name in the register, AtulRastogi, he heard the driver start his car and vanish.

The receptionist was a mild man and pleasantly replied to his question about anyone having enquired about him yet. Andy followed the man, his eyes watchful. There were independent cottages around a central area that had a small garden and a water reservoir where ducks bathed while making a racket. A few children, who surely stayed in these cottages, laughed at the birds. His cottage was right in the end, just as he had requested while booking online.

Soon he was alone. He checked the room quickly and found nothing overtly suspicious. Then he walked back out to the balcony. It was a breath taking sight. The sun was about to sink into the Arabian Sea. In the distance he saw two islands and he was foxed. Both had fort like structures erected on them. One of them was MurudJanjira, the fort that the Siddis protected for five hundred years from foreign invaders, including the Europeans and the Indians. But the question was which one?

The room service boy brought in a cup of tea that Andy had asked for while checking in. The kid had mongoloid features.

'Where are you from?'

'Nepal, sahib.'

Andy opened his wallet and gave him a hundred rupee note. The boy's eyes widened.

'What's your name?'

'Suresh.'

'For how long have you been working here?'

'Two years.'

'I will be here for two days...what's there to see around?'

'Sahib, the beach is good. You can do horse riding there. There is a temple too. And, of course, the fort.'

'Which fort? I can see two from here.'

The boy seemed to be expecting these questions. It was a fact that there was nothing in the vicinity except the forts.

'Sahib, that bigger one is called Janjira and the other one is called the Kasa Fort. Some people also call it Pad-amdurg.' He pointed for the benefit of Andy.

'OK.' Andy recalled that the Kasa Fort had been built by Shivaji when he couldn't conquer Janjira. He knew it was essential to have a presence in the water to keep the Siddis limited to their island.

'Do you serve liquor in your resort?'

The boy shook his head and Andy was surprised. A beach resort without a bar! That was a first.

'I can get you whatever you want from the shop. But you have to hurry as the shops will close in half an hour.'

Andy paid him for half a bottle of Old Monk rum and for a bottle of red wine. He wrote down the brands he wanted in order of preference on the resort's scribbling pad. He didn't want the boy to return empty handed. After the boy was gone, Andy looked back at the sea. The forts had begun to dissolve in the darkness and the water looked black and uninviting. He would have to attempt reaching the fort in this water. The challenge made him want it more.

But for the moment, Andy had reasons to celebrate. He was alive and was going to meet Monica soon. He hoped she had taken all the necessary precautions while arriving at Murud. He would have to be careful. Would she give him away, double cross him? No, it wasn't possible. He knew he could depend on her. Yet he knew most wars were lost due to love and women. Men in love could trust a woman with their lives. And sometimes they realized their blunder only when it was too late. But this wasn't going to happen to him. Like all betrayed heroes, he was certain Monica loved him.

He remembered Karan from the Mahabharata who had faith in everyone and who gave away all that he owned. In return, he got defeat and death. Andy decided to hide a few things from Monica. And since she only knew his name but not his new appearance, he decided to shadow her before revealing himself. This meant that he couldn't stay in the room for long. She would easily make out the room number he was in from his name on the register. Andy washed his hands and face, toweled himself dry and ventured out.

17

Monica was already at Murud. It was perhaps foolish to come here all by herself, but she had faith in Andy. He would protect her, and if he couldn't, she would just accept whatever fate had in store for her.

She wasn't scared of death. If that was her destiny, it had to be for a worthy casue, like trying to help someone who was exposing her villainous boss. She had arrived at Murud a few hours before Andy and was aware of the man outside the resort. He had the impression that she didn't know about his existence. But she was smarter. The man had followed her from the time she left Mumbai airport on a motorcycle.

Was Andy also at the same resort? She had avoided asking for him by his new name as that would have meant exposing him. Instead, Monica walked to the small yellow-walled room that acted as the reception.

She smiled at the lazy man at the table and said, 'Can I please see the booking register?'

The receptionist looked at her and asked why she wanted it.

She said, 'I'm not sure if I have written down the correct dates at the time of checking-in.'

Pleased with her reply, he handed the big register to her and got back to watching his television. Monica settled down on the sofa and began checking the details of guests who had arrived today.

It took her only a second. Atul Rastogi had checked in fifteen minutes ago. His cottage was right next to the one she was staying in. She almost exclaimed in excitement, but controlled herself in the end. Then returning to her calm composure, she handed back the register to the receptionist.

Monica came back to her cottage and saw the man with the bike pretending to read the newspaper, seated in front of a cottage. He had booked himself right opposite to her. He seemed careless. Or he was just acting careless so as to not give her the wrong signals. She got in and closed her door. It was seven in the evening now and the sun had just set. Dusk hung outside, like a promise of a beautiful night ahead and she could hear the waves sweeping the beach right outside the resort.

She had a choice to pick between her boss and Andy

and she had picked Andy. It was an easy choice for her to make and she was prepared to pay any price for her decision. She also realized that she had to stop being so negative about Andy's capabilities in such a sticky situation. Yes, her boss was powerful, but Andy was smarter. He had made the world believe that he was dead, whereas in reality he was very much alive. What was he doing here? What could interest him in such a remote beach town? She had no idea.

There was a knock on the door and she stiffened.

'Room service, Madam.'

But she had not asked for room service. Cautiously opening the door, she said, 'I didn't order anything.'

A young Nepali kid handed her a tray with a cup of tea. A small piece of paper was tucked under the saucer. He left without a word. Monica closed the door, quickly dropped the tray on the table and tore open the paper. It was a message and it said, 'Meet me right now in the central courtyard, near the duck pen.'

The handwritten message ended with the initial AR. She knew who it was. Atul Rastogi.

Monica smiled. All this was adding to the excitement. It was like she was in a movie. The hero was waiting for his lover. And his lover was waiting for an opportunity. And bad people were watching them both, determined not to let it happen. To complete the story, the hero and his lover were united in their cause of exposing a very dirty villain, a depraved enemy of the people and of the nation.

She was about to meet Andy and she wanted to look her best. Monica went to the bathroom and freshened her make-up. But she didn't feel confident of the clothes she was wearing. She took out an evening gown and tried it on. It looked remarkable on her. It enhanced her curves and she shook herself till she thought the gown was holding her body well. Adjusting her posture for the final time, she stepped out of the cottage.

Though it was dark outside, the lamps were enough to see the path. There appeared to be no one outside at that time. Then she saw a family of four returning from the beach. All had black mud marks on them and they smiled at her as they went to their cabin. She knew she was terribly overdressed, but she didn't let it bother her. She had to look her best for Andy. She walked to the duck pen and turned. A man walked past her, limping. Their eyes met only for a moment and she was surprised that he was smiling. She returned his smile feebly and regretted it immediately. There was something in the confidence of the man that made her uncomfortable. Was he too one of KB's men?

When Andy walked past Monica, he was a little surprised at the dress she chose to wear. That would make her stand out at a place like this. She was so obsessed with her looks. But he also knew that she had dressed specially for him and she looked beautiful. It was difficult for anyone to guess her age. She appeared in her early thirties, maybe just a few years older than him.

Earlier, Andy had gone around the resort and discovered all three men who were keeping an eye on Monica. One stayed right opposite her cottage, while two others were outside, walking and chatting. It was the people outside who had alarmed him. He had seen them both at Tilakpur. These were the men who had the opportunity to kill him, but didn't. As he crossed, one of them called him over and asked him for a light. The other stared at him. He smiled and asked them if he could find a girl for the night. They muttered under their breath and he walked away.

These men had, without doubt, followed Monica from Delhi. Did she know about them? He walked to the reception and sat down with a newspaper. From the corner of his eye, he could see Monica dutifully waiting for him. He had noticed the name Ramya in the register while checking-in — her fictitious name.

Andy spoke briefly to the receptionist and learnt that one of the cottages was not being used as its bathroom was under repairs. This could be the best place for them to meet. Or he could slip into Monica's room late at night. The trouble was, if they suddenly crashed open the door and came in, he would have no place to hide. And this time they wouldn't spare his life. He was sure they had the orders to kill anyone they suspected. The enemy was desperate.

He returned to his room and drank two quick pegs of rum. It was quite ironical that though Monica was in the next cottage, he didn't know how to meet her. He thought about his options and decided to call her on the intercom. Andy had already checked that the intercom control was in a room next to the reception and the men following Monica weren't anywhere near it. Under the circumstances, it was safest way for him to get in touch. He had seen her returning to her cottage after waiting for a whole half hour.

'Ramya?'

'Atul?'

'Cottage 8 at 9 pm. Just push the door. I'll be waiting for you in the dark.'

'I have a monkey on my back.'

'You have three. But the one you are worried about will be sedated by then for a few hours and the others are outside. '

'Great. So I'll see you then.'

He heard the click and poured himself another drink. It was easy to sedate the man opposite Monica's cabin. The man had ordered soup and Andy had already taken care of it. Now he had to plan for his early morning visit to the fort.

Before it had turned dark, he had taken a quick ride to the creek where he got the taxi driver to stop earlier and brokered a deal with a fisherman. They were to leave at three in the morning. The man was happy to receive a generous advance and promised not to open his mouth, though he looked surprised. Andy knew fishermen were generally trustworthy people. It was one of the traits they were born with, anywhere in the world. He patted the man on his back and returned.

Now it was all set. The time was eight-thirty. He slipped out of the window in his bathroom and tried to enter cottage number 8 through the same way. But he couldn't. There seemed to be too much rubble inside and the window didn't relent. He walked up to the front, looked around and got inside quickly, pushing the door shut behind him. It made a disquieting noise, so he waited with bated breath and looked out of the window. When he didn't notice any movement for fifteen minutes, his nerves eased a little. He found a fridge in one corner and turned it off. He didn't want the light coming from it to attract anyone's attention. The inside was chilled, indicating that the fridge was working. He placed the red wine bottle and two glasses he was carrying inside it.

It was now five minutes to nine. He sat patiently on the bed. There was no way to know if the bed sheet was clean enough. But as long as there was no unpleasant smell, it didn't matter. Just then, the door opened and he sensed someone come in quietly.

'Atul?'

He heard Monica's voice.

'Monica, over here.'

She ran towards him in the dark. She hugged him and this time he pressed her close. Slowly at first, and then passionately, Andy kissed Monica.

Minutes later he popped the bottle and poured the wine into two glasses.

'Cheers!' he raised a toast.

'Cheers! I missed you...' Monica finished her glass in one go. So did Andy. Then his hands reached for her in the darkness. She guided him inside her dress. Andy fondled her breasts and heard her moan slightly. He kissed her again. She smelt sweet and fresh. He ran his other hand through her hair, moving down to her waist, the curve of her hips and reaching the softness of her thighs. His hands continued their journey and he felt her melt in his arms. Andy was kissing her crazily now, his head moving all over her body. He removed her dress, as she helped him with his, engaging and disengaging to kiss every few seconds in the process. It was a bit awkward, but they were beyond their inhibitions now. Finally, when they were both naked, Andy held her firmly and lowered her on the bed with him on top of her. As he entered her, he heard her moan with pleasure. He felt bulbs of pleasure explode in him every few seconds and his senses were mindlessly excited. Soon he was rocking her faster and faster and finally wildly, with animated passion and energy, both unaware of the sound they were making. When he came it was a rollercoaster of mind-blowing colours that blasted into smithereens and hung in the air for several seconds.

Tired with all the hard work they had put in, both of them fell asleep. Andy woke up with a start and looked at his watch. It was two in the morning. He felt the bed for Monica. She was there, right beside him. He moved his face close to hers and heard her breathing. He touched her hand with his, felt her realize his touch and moan in sleep. Andy shook her lightly and she woke up in his arms.

'I love you!' she whispered.

Andy nodded in the dark. He was undecided if he loved her or it was the desire for sex that had attracted him to this degree.

'We have to go now.'

'Where?'

'You are going to your room and I have work to do.'

'Andy, I wanted to tell you that KB has something to do with whatever you are doing. He showed me your photographs with an old man who looked every bit government. Just tell me what is going on? Who are you, really?'

He stayed quiet. He knew he could trust her, but intelligence matters were only shared on a need-to-know basis. He didn't want to burden her with unnecessary information. But he was surprised that KB was keeping such a close watch on him. He was having him followed and even knew that he was in Mumbai. The man was corrupt and somehow he was connected to Murud Janjira. If he was lucky he would be able to figure the link before sunrise.

'Don't tell me if you don't want to,' she said softly and in response he embraced her. They held each other and stayed like that for a long time, feeling the warmth of each other's breath on their shoulders.

'Be careful!' she finally whispered and he replied, 'You too...'

Slowly, they made their way out of the room. It was colder and Monica instinctively folded into him. He urged her to move quickly and they reached their cottages in the cover of darkness. Visibility was less than ten feet and no one seemed to have noticed them. No doors opened, no lights were turned on. All they could hear was the sound of the waves crashing tirelessly on the beach.

After he was alone in his room, Andy changed into tight pants and boots he had brought from Mumbai. The Commissioner had mentioned scorpions and snakes and he was not taking any chances. Andy slipped out and waited under a mango tree, searching for the two men he had seen earlier. He couldn't see them. He began walking towards the creek, hoping for a vehicle to cross him. Ten minutes later he saw lights and waved frantically for it to stop. A truck slowed down next to him and a drunken Sardar beamed happily at him.

'Kithhe?'

Andy liked Sardars. They were fun loving, made jokes about themselves and spoke in their own language with everyone, irrespective of where they were in the world.

'About twenty kilometres, Paaji!'

The Sardar smiled and began with the story of his life. He had a wife and six children. The children were like him and loved drinking Scotch.

'Scotch?' Andy wondered if he was mad, giving alcohol to his children.

'All children in Punjab drink a lot of Scotch.'

It was only after a few more sentences that Andy realized that the Sardar meant 'squash' and his pronunciation made it sound like 'Scotch'.

He got down after a few more minutes and offered some money to the jovial Sardar for the ride. The burly driver refused and drove off into the night towards the city.

Andy found the fisherman waiting. The boat was ready. The anchor had been taken off and now the boat was tied on two stout logs that stood out from under the water. Fortunately for them it was high tide. He smiled at the fisherman and climbed into the boat. The man pushed it for a short distance and when he was in knee deep water, he jumped on board. Using a long stick, he pushed the boat clear of the creek and towards the sea.

It took them fifteen minutes to reach the creek's mouth and once they were there, the man started the small diesel engine. It coughed and started in the third attempt. The silence was now broken by a gentle sound from the engine.

'Where do you want to go?' the fisherman asked him.

'Janjira.'

'No use. There'll be no one there at this time.'

'Janjira.' Andy repeated. The man turned the tiller and the rudder swung the boat to the left. They were now moving south. The coast was to their left and he could see the faint shoreline. Janjira Fort was not visible as it was still some distance away.

There were a few fishing boats around them and their lights simmered in the night, reflecting on the gentle waves of the Arabian Sea. The sky was moonless and the stars shone brightly. Andy knew the best place to observe the magic of the stars was always from the sea. In fact, during earlier voyages, mariners used them to navigate, equipped with logarithmic tables and a sextant.

They sailed in silence. Andy told the man that he needed the boat for only four hours. It meant he could use it till seven in the morning. But he was hoping to let him off much sooner. At about four, the man pointed the outline of Janjira Fort to Andy. There were three boats fishing not far from the fort island.

They continued towards Janjira. When their boat was about a hundred metres away, Andy asked for the engine to be stopped and the single masthead light that ran on the boat's battery to be switched off. The two of them then began to row in the darkness. The only sound was from the oars splashing in and out of the water.

Andy's view got better and better as he neared the fort. The wall seemed to rise higher as they came closer. Now he could see why Shivaji and all the European navies were unsuccessful in scaling these walls. The walls seemed higher than twelve metres, though according to the guide books, they were factually twelve. There was no recess anywhere on the wall, no place from where one could get a grip to climb. Slowing, lapping water and ensuring that minimum sound was made, they began to circle the island. When they reached the rear, Andy saw the rabbit gate. Ingress looked possible here as the wall had a few cracks. He put his foot in one of the cracks and pulled himself out of the boat. Once he was comfortable, he waved the boat away. He had already told the fisherman to meet him exactly after ninety minutes at the same spot.

18

Andy climbed the wall with relative ease. It wasn't too difficult. He got into the fort using the rabbit gate. There was thick vegetation in front of him and just as he was wondering how best to gain access, he heard someone sneeze. It seemed to come from not too far away. Perhaps a hundred feet at the most. He knew that sound travelled longer distances at night. But at least one thing was clear — there was someone else on the island besides him. Was that man alone? Surely not! Hakim had mentioned explosives. It seemed almost certain that this was the place the enemy was using to hide those explosives.

He moved a few branches and his foot fell on something soft. He jumped back. It was like an animal resting there. Did he step on a python? He moved quickly and stood in the clearing on the wall. If it was a python, he would see it coming. Amongst the trees he was like a sitting duck. Andy waited for ten minutes and when nothing happened, he slowly reached the same spot, this time his pistol drawn. Though he knew using a pistol would mean giving away his location, but at least he could save his life with it and then escape in the boat.

He felt the same softness under his feet once again. He bent down and touched it with his hand. It felt like rubber, inflated rubber. It was a dingy. Yes, he thought, a dingy near the escape gate. He should have thought of that. There were people inside and they had their dingy ready to escape. Andy's first reaction was to puncture it, but doing that would just warn the people inside. They would know that someone had come and they would think of other means to escape — and also actually escape instead of waiting for Andy to return with reinforcements. No, he had to give it some more thought. He needed to catch these guys unawares.

Andy tried to gain access through the shrubs, but couldn't. The Commissioner was right. The vegetation was so thick that it was practically impenetrable. He came back and walked on the wall, keeping low and moved towards the source of the sound. The wall was circular and that would keep him out of sight if someone was watching. Until he came close. Once he approached the side that faced the coast, he slowed down. This was where he hoped the man on the watch would be. By the time he spotted the man, he was crawling on the wall, his elbows and knees bruised. He stopped in the distance and spotted a man yawning uncontrollably. It looked like he would drop off to dreamland shortly.

Andy retraced his steps. There was nothing he could do now. He was alone and vulnerable. His mission though, was over. He scrambled back towards the rabbit gate, climbed down the walls using the crack and began to wait for the boat. The boat appeared on time and he jumped into it. They rowed away from the fort and then started the engine. Dawn had started to break as they reached the creek. Andy paid the fisherman the balance money and said he might come again at night. The man nodded in understanding.

Monica couldn't sleep after she reached her room. It was for the first time that someone had made love to her because he wanted to. Andy had loved her in the dark room, not used her body for sex. She felt complete and cared for. Now, for the first time in her life, she had a lover. A real lover. She had never imagined life could take such a beautiful turn. She wasn't thinking about why Andy had not responded to her 'I love you.' As a woman, she could sense that Andy was in love with her. There was no mistaking that. She knew it wouldn't be long before Andy would profess his love for her. Monica had finally found happiness. She thought that even if she died at this moment she wouldn't have any regrets.

There was a sound at the door. Perhaps Andy was

back. She smiled in the dark. Seconds later, rough hands covered her mouth as she struggled. More hands grabbed her body and brought her under control. She writhed in pain and wasn't able to breathe. Two men were strangling her. She moved her body with all her might, but her attackers were more powerful. She hoped like hell for Andy to appear and kill these bastards. But no one came to help. Slowly she sank deeper and deeper into the darkness that was ushering her in. Her body stopped moving after one final wild attempt. Then she turned cold. The rough hands left her. Now it was all quiet.

When the morning light lit her room, Monica was staring at the ceiling, her eyes still open. There were marks from Andy's stubble on her face. She looked relaxed and contented.

The reception called the police. They arrived in half an hour and starting asking questions. Andy was sleeping peacefully in his cottage when he heard the commotion outside. Out of curiosity, he came out and was surprised to see people gathered in front of Monica's cottage. He rushed towards them. His worst fears were confirmed when he came to know that the lady there was murdered.

He couldn't stand there any more and dashed to his room. Once inside, he sank on his knees. Ever since losing his mother, he had never felt such grief. There was no one in the world he could share his sorrow with.

The curse of his name would never leave him. Andy

pressed his temples.

Your name is Karan and you can never win. Whatever you love will be taken from you. You are cursed, Karan. You are a good person, yet you are cursed.

It took him an hour to get his bearings straight. Whoever had killed Monica would pay dearly. He would find out and kill him mercilessly. He knew this was against the law, but nothing mattered any more.

Andy got up from the bed. There was no time for remorse. The enemy was out there, successful in slowing him down, successful in dampening his spirit to fight. But he wouldn't let that happen. He organized his thoughts and realized that he could only avenge Monica's death if he stayed focused.

When the Commissioner called, Andy informed him about Monica's murder.

The Commissioner assured him, 'Sorry to hear that, but don't worry. You won't be bothered with the police interrogation. Please stay focused on the purpose of your visit.'

He also promised to get a thorough investigation done and catch the murderers soon.

'Hakim was right. They are in Janjira. I was there before sunrise and saw them myself.' Andy shared the details of his visit.

'I'm embarrassed that my team could not find any-thing.'

Andy said in the end, 'I want to go back to the island with the police. There might be resistance. We have very little time.'

The Commissioner agreed immediately.

They planned the takeover of the island on the same night. Andy and eight of Mumbai's finest made the team. Andy told them of his plan and they nodded. They were connected to each other through the radio embedded in their helmets. Andy confirmed the call signs with them and they rehearsed as the team headed to the creek at midnight.

Abdul's man wasn't drowsy. He had seen Andy crawling on the wall. But he feigned ignorance and yawned to mis-lead him. As Andy retracted towards the rear of the fort, the man followed him. When Andy jumped into the boat, he peeped below, the black wall working as stealth behind him. He knew Andy would not be able to see him, but he carefully noted Andy jumping on to the fishing boat. With experience, the man knew that this visit was a prac-tice run. He checked the rubber dingy and quickly went down to the chamber where Abdul worked with the oth-ers.

Abdul was upset. He just needed a few more hours to

get the work done. But he knew the enemy could attack any time during the following day or night. They had to dismantle everything and escape as quickly as possible. He ordered the emergency procedure the team had practised earlier and passed the information on to Kismet Khan, his boss. His plan was approved, but he was asked not to destroy the bomb — at least for the time being.

An hour later they removed whatever they could and moved towards the boat, Abdul holding the bomb in his hands. The nuclear core was still unstable and therefore, they had to be doubly careful. Any jerk and the bomb would detonate. Once at the rabbit gate, they slid the rubber dingy into water, fitted the OBM, picked the additional petrol tanks and got in. Abdul kept the bomb in the centre. He looked at the island one final time, his home for the last six months, took a long breath and ordered the OBM to be started.

Soon they were cruising towards the coast. Kismet Khan had already told them where to go. It was seven in the morning and the sea was calm. The calmness of the sea kept the boat steady as they neared the shoreline. The bomb stayed safe for now.

They reached a minor fishing harbour where a man who said his name was Kasim bhai received them. He had driven down in a Mahindra Scorpio. The bomb was kept safely on the middle seat and Abdul explained to Kasim bhai, 'You have to drive very carefully. Even the slightest jerk could destroy our goods.'

Kasim bhai was a lean Gujarati who kept chewing his *paan* and replied, 'Of course, I understand.'

But the fact was he didn't and drove carelessly from the word go.

Abdul didn't give him a second chance. In their profession, the first mistake was always the last mistake. He asked him to pull over to one side, shot him from point blank range, hid his body in the nearby bushes and ordered one of his men to drive towards Mumbai. They were in a desperate situation and there was no scope for error.

Abdul wanted to cover the maximum distance he possibly could before the police realized that they had missed their bus. As they drove on, he realized his immediate problems. One was the lack of communication with Kismet Khan as he had already destroyed the satellite phone at Janjira Fort and left the fragmented remains there. The second problem was reaching their destination and establishing contact with the person who would accept the merchandise, the bomb, from them. Finally, his third problem was reaching Pakistan after the mission.

He had taken the Gujarati's cell phone and was hoping to use it to speak to Kismet Khan one final time. But he knew, just as he needed time to work out his plan, Kismet Khan also needed to iron out the kinks in his own. He decided to call after a few hours.

Andy reached the island after midnight with the police crack team. The first thing he discovered was the missing dingy. He walked his team along the wall and discovered that his worst fears had been realized. The lookout — the drowsy man — was gone too. They searched for hours on the deserted island but there was no trace of the enemy.

As sunrise cracked the eastern sky to a crimson horizon and as daylight grew around them, they found an obscure footpath leading into the fort. The light made it easier to navigate their way and they reached the bottom cavern in ten minutes. Once inside the fort, it took them another hour to find the way to the chamber located underneath the fresh water tank.

Andy and his team descended into its cold interiors. Furniture was strewn all around. This was for the second time since Tilakpur that the enemy had guessed their move and disappeared hours before they could reach. He saw the burnt satellite phone and knew of the international connection.

Andy called the Commissioner and told him the entire situation. The Commissioner had bad news to share too. Mr Kapoor had died. But he had left behind a report. 'To be opened only on my death.' These words were super-scribed on an envelope that was found in the locker at his office in North Block. The contents made it clear to the government that Andy was working for them. The Commissioner expressed his regret that he had doubted

Andy's intentions when he met him for the first time at the Police HQ in Mumbai.

There was also another message for him, which the Commissioner conveyed at once. He had been asked to report back to Delhi. Andy first needed to get off the island. Instead of the creek, they sailed back to Murud jetty this time and berthed at the fishing harbour. Andy paid the fisherman. He checked-out of the resort immediately on arrival and left with a police escort to Mumbai.

Monica was cremated the previous evening. There was no one they could trace back as her family. The pyre was lit by a policeman as Andy watched along with a few unknown people from the resort. They slowly drifted away as he stood at the open crematorium for a long time, engulfed in the smoke and the sadness. The woman he held in his arms last night had now been reduced to a few burning embers that refused to die out. Just like Monica.

Andy walked back to the cottage where Monica had spent the last few hours of her life. A lone policeman stood guard at the entrance. After some persuasion, Andy was able to smooth talk his way in to check on a few things. His acquaintance with the Police Commissioner also helped a great deal.

The room still smelt of Monica. The police had kept her items on the bed. There was no claimant. He picked up her purse and emptied its contents. Numerous cosmetic tubes, two key chains and a peppermint packet fell out. There was a smaller wallet too. He opened it. There were a few thousand rupee notes and a credit card. He found a photograph in one of its inner pockets. It was his picture. Monica was so fond of him that she kept his picture in her purse. Yet it took her such a long time to convey these feelings to him!

He also found a small diary and pocketed it after leafing through the pages briefly. It was a diary she wrote in regularly. There were names in it, her daily meetings and some notes. Maybe this would help him understand why Monica behaved differently in the beginning when she sent him to Tilakpur.

Her clothes were neatly arranged in hangers in the closet, as if she had hoped to stay a few days at the resort. It would take a long time for Andy to get over Monica's loss. He knew he had to find her killer. He owed it to her, to someone who loved him unconditionally and risked her own life to save him.

19

Abdul knew he had to avoid the main roads as his vehicle moved north. Check points were expected after every few kilometres and their luck could run out at any one of them. For starters, their accent would give them away. It was at about four in the evening that he received his final orders from Kismet Khan. The merchandise was to be taken through the state of Rajasthan into Haryana and handed over to a man called Sultan Shaitan at a small village called Tilakpur.

Sultan Shaitan had the alphabets 'SS' tattooed on his right forearm, he was informed so that he could identify Shaitan on reaching his destination. This was important and he made a mental note of it. Immediately after the delivery all four of them were required to head for the Nepal border and cross over. Further instructions would be given after they arrived in Pokhran, Nepal. Kismet Khan wished him luck for the mission and asked him to take every precaution.

Abdul had bought a road map from a small shop at a town they had crossed a few hours back. He consulted it as their SUV moved at a steady speed. He was taking the interior roads for safety. It was unlikely that they'd be nabbed on these roads. But these roads were severely broken and potholed and they were losing a lot of time as they couldn't drive fast. The bomb was the other problem. Abdul sat with the bomb, his baby, in the lap, his body absorbing the shocks of the vehicle as much as was possible. As they went through a rather harsh bump, he barked, 'Slow down, you idiot!'

'I'm doing the best I can,' the driver whispered through clenched teeth.

Abdul took out his pistol and pointed at the man's head. He continued driving, his mouth open in surprise.

'I'll make a pothole in your head if you ever speak to me like that again. Clear?'

The man at the wheel nodded. They drove in silence, Abdul concentrating on the map and the others staring blankly at the road in front of them.

About nine hundred kilometres north of them, Krishna Bedi relaxed in his farm house. He was reading a newspaper. He had every reason to feel content. Monica had been killed and the bomb was on its way to him. The dirty bomb for dirty politicians, he relished the thought. He set the paper aside and smiled.

KB had three idols in the world. One was Hitler, the person who fought till his last breath to pursue his dream of ruling the world. He liked the immensity of his ambition and his ruthlessness to achieve it. It was sad that he failed in the end. But KB adored him because he tried.

The others were the Vietnamese and the North Koreans. The Vietnamese had given the Americans a good fight in the 1970s and never gave up, despite being weak on every front: technology, training, experience in warfare, and weapons. But they had something special that the Americans didn't possess— courage. This alone drove the enemies from their shore. The North Koreans were his favourites as of now. They were not scared of anyone in the world. They were patriotic and courageous. America was threatening them every single day, daring them not to build nuclear weapons despite having so many in its own arsenal. But they were not giving up in the face of sure defeat. They had balls. Just like Hitler and the Vietnamese.

The fact was KB liked people with balls, the balls which he thought he had in good measure, but the people who ran the country didn't. They were throwing the country to the Americans and the Europeans. He had to teach them a lesson. He had to rescue his nation from these cowards who were mere slaves of Western influence and money.

A bomb was the best weapon with which he could

achieve all of this. He would start with his secret mission the moment he took delivery of the bomb. The Prime Minister would surely chicken out and make the policy changes that he wanted. That would divert many contracts to him, while the Americans and the Europeans would be left sucking their thumbs. KB couldn't stop beaming just by thinking about it. But he settled down immediately, he reminded himself that he had to concentrate on some finer details pertaining to the bomb before implementation. Kismet Khan had said it would be safe at Tilakpur. But KB knew it wouldn't. Suddenly, he knew a place where it would be the safest — his house.

He used his links to get through to the Home Secretary, who agreed for a meeting in the evening at five. The ball had started to roll. His future was all set. He laughed once again and the sound travelled through all his rooms and returned to him in a humble echo.

By the time Andy landed at IGI, the nation's capital had geared itself for the worst. But it wasn't visible to him, or to the common people. The madness on the roads, the ceaseless honking, the translucency of the milky fog, it was just a typical winter day. Andy's taxi pretty nearly rode over a calf that came out on the road from nowhere, but other than that his ride was uneventful.

Andy had asked the driver to take him to a friend's house. It was dangerous to go home. He remembered the

neat bullet holes in the door of his house. As the car negotiated the traffic on Ring Road, he wondered why Monica
was killed. She had warned him in Mumbai seconds before a big man was about to reach for his neck. From what
she said, he recalled, it appeared that their enemy was the
same. Who was this person who held all the strings?

Many had lost their lives. At Tilakpur, the lawyer, the
police constable who was his best friend, and Gulabo.
In Mumbai, the informer Hakim. In Delhi, the master
planner, Mr Kapoor himself. And at Murud, the beautiful Monica. The enemy was smart and knew all his moves
beforehand. When he visited Tilakpur, they were ready
for him. When he arrived in Mumbai, they were expecting him. And before he could reach Janjira Fort, they had
bid it farewell. Did the enemy know that he had reached
Delhi? He looked outside the window in desperation, feeling stupid and vulnerable.

His thoughts took him back to Monica. She had been
uncertain from the start. She knew of the dangers. She
knew more than him and had been hiding something.
Did she know who was behind this whole operation? She
had told him to be careful about KB. But why would a successful businessman help the terrorists? What was there in
it for him?

He remembered the diary. He took it out from his pocket and began flipping through the pages. Even in this age of
the internet and smart phone memos, Monica was regular

with her diary. He read snippets from her life: her parlour experiences, the movies she liked, the new wines she had tried, the money she spent on charities. He was touched. She indeed had a heart of gold. The world had not treated her well and yet she had given the world her all.

The taxi reached its destination. He closed the diary and kept it back safely. As he alighted, the big lock on the door conveyed that his friend was not at home. Andy wondered where to go next. He decided to go into the crowds. More the people, the safer he would be. So he asked the driver to take him to Paharganj. He checked into a cheap hotel there.

As he lay down in bed, Andy thought of Krishna Bedi. He had seen him on the television and though he knew that the magazine was owned by him, the man had never visited the office while Andy was around. Monica too never spoke about him. The chances of his involvement were less as he was rich and he had no possible reason to go on a killing spree or even worse, betray his country. He pushed the thought out of his mind and replayed everything that had happened, right from the time he first visited Tilakpur in his head. He still couldn't connect the dots. Andy decided to get some sleep.

Andy woke with a start. His phone was ringing. No one except the Commissioner and Monica knew about this number and since Monica was dead, this call had to be coming from Mumbai. He blinked at the clock. It was four.

'Hello!' He sounded groggy.

'Is this Andy Karan?'

It was a voice he had never heard before. He sat up in the bed. The man at the other end asked again.

'Maybe...'

'You are wanted right now. The National Security Advisor needs you.'

'Yeah, fuck you too, buddy!'

Andy hung up, removed the battery from the phone and went back to sleep. He was not going to be tricked any more. He would finish it all by himself. He tried, but sleep was a distant dream now. What little he managed was even worse than staying awake, for all he dreamt about was flying in the air with a bomb, which eventually blew up and...

Andy jumped out of bed. He heard it again. A vehicle's door just slammed shut.

He ran up to the window and peeped out from behind the curtains. He saw three men in black suits walk away from a black SUV parked at the mouth of the alley. They looked professional, tall men who walked on springy legs. Andy knew it. His phone had given his location away. He grabbed his stuff and opened the door. Sounds of steps reached him from the floor below and he ran up a flight, making sure he didn't make any noise. He expected them to enter his room and search for him before bolting out in panic on not finding him. He had around a thirty second lead. Was it going to be enough?

He reached the roof. The buildings were close enough for him to jump across. But he ran in the darkness till he reached the edge of the building. He didn't want to spend too much time running on rooftops. They'd just outnumber him till he ran out of roofs. Andy instead crossed over to the little ledge on the exterior side of the building and used the water pipes to slide down. Buildings in Paharganj were thankfully small.

As soon as Andy's feet hit the pavement, he snapped around on his heels and jumped into the narrow back alley behind the hotel building he was staying in. He kept walking for ten minutes.

He paused and looked around. It was a narrow alley. There were dogs, humans and waste, all lying side by side in that dingy little cramped pathway. Just when he thought he had managed to give them a slip, he felt someone touch his shoulder and he stiffened. Two men came from behind. Andy threw a punch to his left, but the suit was faster. He quickly ducked out of the path of Andy's fist and this gave the other suit enough time to grab Andy by the neck and push him up against the wall. Andy tried desperately to wriggle free, but his attackers had a strong hold on him, till they slapped handcuffs on him.

'We didn't want to use force, Sir, but you're one hell

of a customer.' The man's voice was replete with sarcasm.

He was told they worked for the government. Two of them were from the NSG and one was a Delhi Police commando. Andy realized why they called him 'Sir'. Not just were the three of them younger than him, they were all his juniors in the armed services. Andy relaxed and resigned himself to a drive to South Block. They removed his handcuffs on the way.

South Block, together with the Rashtrapati Bhawan and North Block, is an imposing building from where the Indian Government conducts its security, strategy and financial business. Constructed with red and cream Dholpur stone from Rajasthan, it was designed by the British architect Herbert Baker, second-in-command to Sir Edwin Lutyens, who designed 'New' Delhi. It is identical to the North Block, with a dome at the top. There are four floors, each with 1000 interconnected rooms and wide corridors and staircases. All the floors end into colonnaded balconies on its four sides. While the South block houses the Ministry of Defence and External Affairs, North Block is the seat of the Home and Finance ministries.

The car soon cut across Raj Path and the imposing structure stood out majestically against the dark sky like a bear getting up to hunt. As Andy got down, he saw light falling on the lawn below through a *chatri* on the third floor. The four of them passed a massive gate. The men showed the heavily armed sentry their ID cards and entered a lift which had sliding, collapsible metal doors.

The lift took them to a dark corridor, the end of which was brightly lit.

'This way, Sir!' one of them said and they continued walking.

Andy entered a huge conference hall, while his escorts stayed out. It was a big rectangular room with a heavy mahogany table with ornamental legs resting in the centre. Leather upholstered chairs were pushed against it on all its sides. Six of them were occupied by old men, cups of tea and biscuits in front of them. One of them rose and walked up to Andy. He extended his hand and Andy shook it, his smile half-hearted. He felt the power these men possessed.

'I'm Bhushan Singh, NSA to the Prime Minister.'

'Andy Karan.'

'I know.' He pulled a chair and Andy sat in it. It was like sitting on a cloud. The chair accepted his weight and he slowly sank into it. Perhaps for about three seconds. A waiter appeared through the door and brought him a cup of tea.

'OK, so let's not waste any time. Andy, you know the ministers...there's Defence, Home and External Affairs. Together we form the National Security Council. As you already know, we have a bomb coming our way. This is no ordinary bomb, it's a dirty bomb. You, of course know what that means, right?'

Andy just nodded, letting every word sink in.

'Let me share a few facts that you may not know. The NIA is at Murud as we speak, and the NTRO is monitoring the situation via satellite. Minor nuclear traces have been found at Murud. Cesium 137. It's an isotope of Uranium that emits gamma radiation. It's highly reactive and can contaminate anything that comes in its way. Our protection is only cement, lead and steel.'

He paused, looked at the ministers who heard him out without any reaction to the National Intelligence Agency and the National Technical Research Organization reports, took a sip of tea from his cup and continued, 'We can't ignore this bomb. We have to protect the city.'

Andy nodded. He knew Cesuim 137 radiation exposure could induce Acute Radiation Syndrome, ARD as it was called, which caused redness of skin, huge chunks of hair fall, itching and flaking of skin within hours. The contaminated person would die in a few weeks, or months, depending on the degree of exposure. For those lucky to survive, the recovery could take up to two years. And of course, there was another problem. It was contagious.

There was pin-drop silence in the seat of Indian power. The Defence Minister got up and came closer. He whispered, 'Son, we want to know what else we have missed.

You seem to be right in the middle of all this. Mr Kapoor is gone, but he had left a good note on you and we are very impressed with what you have done for us till now.'

'Sir, I'm just doing the job I had promised the day I left the Army.'

'Of course you are, and you will be rewarded for your services. But right now you have to help us. What do you think we must do? Where do we even begin?'

Andy was surprised. The country's top Security Council which reported to the Prime Minister directly, wanted to know from him what could be done. They seemed desperate.

The NSA continued, 'You must have heard of Krishna Bedi.'

Andy nodded once again. 'Yes. He owns the magazine I work for.'

'He met the Prime Minister today and he said he has the bomb. He is blackmailing us.'

Andy's jaw dropped. He remembered Monica's warnings about KB and his sudden interest in him. So it really had been KB all along.

But there was more. 'He has placed some demands... the type of demands we cannot possibly accept as it would destroy the nation. The ultimatum is till 5 pm tomorrow.'

Andy was exasperated. How did the bomb reach Delhi? It wasn't possible to fly the thing, or bring on a train. The only other way was by road and less than forty-eight hours had elapsed, definitely not sufficient time enough for someone to drive almost 2000 kms with an unstable nuclear bomb.

'He's bluffing. The bomb couldn't have reached him so fast.'

'I agree. We have already sealed all the Delhi borders. Everything is being checked and in case of doubt people are being sent back. We have check posts now at every fifty kilometres all the way from Delhi to Mumbai, on every possible route.'

Andy was thinking. Bhushan Singh continued, 'But we have to believe him. What if he has the bomb? What if he got it from elsewhere, not from Murud? We can't wait till tomorrow evening to know whether he is indeed speaking the truth!'

Andy felt that the desire to stay in power had turned these politicians weak. He pitied their condition. They had no risk taking capability. They had been clueless all along, and now when they knew of the situation, they had no idea what to do. Politicians, he thought, irritated, only knew what could not be done. It was time he took the initiative. He didn't particularly like taking such a huge responsibility, but someone would have to do something about it.

'All right, gentlemen! Here is what we should do...' He told them his impromptu plan. They all agreed instantly that this was the only thing to do.

Andy walked out and the waiting soldiers followed him to the SUV. He didn't speak to them. They were merely escorts. Back at the hotel, Andy bid them farewell and reclined on his bed in deep thought.

They had told him where KB stayed. But where was the bomb at this very moment? He desperately wanted to sleep, but was worried that he wouldn't have enough time to stop the bomb from going off. He had a plan now, and though it looked pretty impossible to achieve at the moment, he knew it was the only option they had.

20

Abdul was successful in avoiding the last check-post on the highway. He had ordered the driver to turn the Scorpio back, entered a village that was adjacent to the road and emerged a few hundred metres on the other side of the post after driving through a field. It was a crude method and their vehicle bumped and swerved wildly every few metres. They finally reached the road and the smooth pitch calmed their nerves to some extent. He knew he had gotten lucky this time, but he'd have to think of a better way.

After a kilometre he ordered the vehicle to be stopped. They were on a lonely stretch and he asked everyone to get down.

He said, 'It's time for a special prayer. We need to thank the Almighty for protecting us this far and ask him to be with us for the rest of our journey.'

The four of them walked to one side and sat down on the grass to pray. There were Acacia trees and thorny bushes all around them. In one swift motion, Abdul took out his pistol and shot two of them dead. As Abdul dragged the bodies behind the bushes, the one whom he had kept alive shook like a leaf stuck on a window pane on a stormy night.

At the next village, Abdul bought women's clothes and cosmetics. He handed over a pair to his assistant and said, 'Dress up. Fast!'

The poor man, who was about twenty years old, was still dazed with the murder of his two colleagues. He knew better than to question Abdul's orders.

They changed in the Scorpio. Dressed as women they walked towards the road, abandoning their vehicle. By now, Abdul imagined, the police would have discovered Kasim bhai's body.

The two of them reached the road and stood uncertainly, hoping to get a lift. But no one stopped for them. People who crossed wore disgusted expressions and a few stuck their heads out and abused them. Abdul saw a truck approaching and waved his hands frantically for it to stop.

A burly Sardar was at the wheel. He allowed them to get into his truck. When Abdul started to climb in, the driver instructed, 'Let the younger one come in first.' Abdul nodded. He understood the reason for this favour.

'I'm going to Chandigarh. Where do you want to go?' The Sardar was drinking straight from the bottle.

Abdul said in a softer voice, 'Drop us outside Delhi, if you please. We will pay you for the lift.'

The Sardar beamed. 'No, no! I'm going in the same direction.'

Abdul's assistant looked prettier and he noticed the Sardar taking a fancy to him. It was a good sign. He hid the suitcase under the seat and said, 'Please drive slowly if you can. She gets very giddy in fast vehicles.'

But the Sardar continued without any effect. Abdul nudged his assistant. He still seemed shaken and looked at Abdul in alarm. He motioned with his head towards the driver.

The young man whispered, 'Please drive slowly...I'm not feeling too well already.'

The Sardar smiled this time and immediately reduced his speed considerably.

Abdul knew turning into *hijras* worked for them in two ways. One, their features were adequately camouflaged, and two, the police would not take them seriously and they might escape a thorough scrutiny. It worked exactly as he had hoped and soon they were on the NH 8, cruising towards Delhi.

They arrived at Gurgaon the next day. KB's instructions were already waiting for them. The entire drive had been a test of patience and Abdul was satisfied the way he had handled it.

It wasn't very difficult for them to reach Chhatarpur from Gurgaon. They came on foot through the vast fields spread around the area and stayed away from the road. Once at the farmhouse, they jumped the back wall as advised by KB, to avoid being seen by the policemen who were watching the entrance. It was almost midnight.

KB was already expecting them and received them happily. He heard their story as they told him how difficult it was to transport the bomb safely to him. He offered both the most expensive whisky and hosted a feast fit for kings in their honour, after they had washed and changed. Once dinner was over, Abdul said they wanted to rest as they were very tired.

KB insisted on some more whisky, while he explained his plans to them in detail. Soon they started to feel unwell. After five minutes, KB stopped speaking. He waited as they wallowed on the floor, incapacitated, holding their stomachs tightly.

They were dead soon. KB got them buried behind the house. In the same grave he threw the SIM card he had used to communicate with Kismet Khan for the past six months. Now he didn't need Kismet Khan's help anymore. KB had the bomb and he saw it as a money making machine for himself. He was at the top of the world. After all the killings and sleepless nights, things were finally in his control now.

The meeting with the Home Secretary had proceeded as per plan and the scared bureaucrat had taken him to the Prime Minister as soon as he heard about the bomb.

The Prime Minister stared at him with a shocked expression. 'Are you out of your mind?' he had said.

But KB knew it was exactly the opposite. He told him that and the head of the nation held his temples in despair. KB felt the power surging through him. Even without the support of the people, he realized that at that moment he literally owned the country through someone whom the people had elected. Everything was easy in a democracy. One needed money and everything else fell into place. Like now.

After a few minutes, the Prime Minister pleaded, 'Your demands will be met. Please don't think of using the bomb.'

KB promised with childlike innocence that he wouldn't; but if he was ditched, he would be left without a choice.

'Dirty bomb for dirty politics,' he whispered, got up and walked away leaving a baffled old man looking tinier behind a huge Victorian desk.

After his return, with the help of his most trusted assistant, KB placed the bomb gently in the bedroom. It was the perfect place. While he slept at night, he didn't want to be away from his most wonderful possession. He had fallen in love with the bomb. It was better than falling in love with a woman. It was absolute, selfless and unconditional. He dreamt of a life with more money and the whole world at his disposal.

He had given the responsibility of the security of his farm to his most trusted henchman, Sultan Shaitan. He was pleased with how Shaitan had handled the Tilakpur cell successfully for the past two years and removed all the trouble makers: Gulabo and her husband, Andy, Monica, Mr Kapoor and Hakim. He had followed orders to the T and there were no mistakes. Not even a stray hit man, whom a property dealer had hired to eliminate Ram Avtar, was spared. Of course, at that time they were not aware that the man in the black kurta pajama following Ram Avtar was a small time contract killer. If there was one man KB could trust his life with, it was Shaitan. In the past ten years, he had helped KB tide over many such sticky situations.

KB embraced the suitcase with the bomb, kissed it and fell asleep, thinking of all the money he was about to snatch from the mouths of the Western companies, the wily conspirators who had brainwashed the Government and the nation.

But the very next morning he was in for an ugly

surprise. As per Andy's plan, KB was informed that the Prime Minister couldn't accept his demands. A furious KB shouted at them and asked them to get ready to go down in history as the killers of thousands of innocent people.

In the early hours of the morning, a curfew had been imposed in Delhi. The main arterial roads coming into the capital from Haryana and Uttar Pradesh were barricaded. No one was allowed to cross these barriers which were manned by heavily armed personnel. No VVIPs, no red beacon cars, no one! In the capital, people were advised to stay calm, but indoors. CISF, Army and Delhi Police platoons had been deployed on most roads. Delhi had turned into a fortress overnight.

The media was asked to show restraint and not report any incident without properly corroborating with the police. Andy had reminded them of the errors the media had committed during the Mumbai attacks of 2008. He said, before the media gets restless, it was prudent that the government inform the people of the situation, so as to curb rumour mills and nasty speculations.

Andy was surprised that they were following his plan completely. The nation had many intelligence gathering agencies, many organizations to analyse raw data and research them out, but no one wanted to take any action on these findings — Andy felt pretty irritated with this mentality. He had become their action arrowhead. The nation depended on his plan. He felt the weight of the responsibility on his shoulders. Ordinary citizens had elected politicians who had elected him for this job, an ordinary citizen. It was, like everything else in the world, a full circle.

KB had given the ultimatum that the bomb would explode at 5 pm if his demands were not met. Now that they had decided not to get blackmailed by him, the disaster could strike anywhere: markets, roads, buildings, monuments, democratic institutions, anywhere. As the day progressed, speculation began to spread and as planned, the Home Minister came on air. He looked solemn, the Indian flag behind him and the picture of Mahatma Gandhi on his side.

In a deep voice, he read: 'There is a threat of a terrorist strike in Delhi. It could be in any locality. But as long as everyone follows the instructions of the government and stay indoors, everything will be fine. Thank you.' All television and radio stations broadcasted it live.

Despite his statement, the media began to speculate. One said there might be a war, citing previous situations like this in other countries. Another said a coup was probably the reason for the people to be kept indoors.

The uniformed police and paramilitary personnel were guarding all the roads as if their lives depended on it. Certain parts of the capital were under the control of the Army. A few incidents of stone pelting by people from terraces in some areas occurred, but it was brought under control by firing warning shots in the air by the police. In one locality, police had to fire rubber bullets on people to ensure that the group of protesters that had swelled to ten shouldn't increase. A large group could derail the entire security measure. One person died in the scuffle, but the others receded out of sight.

There was palpable unrest. It was almost impossible to keep ten million people on a leash. But the government had no other option. They could not clearly inform the citizens what the situation was. All deployed platoon commanders had been given shoot-on-sight orders if their efforts to warn failed. It was like an Emergency.

No one knew from where the bomb would enter the city. They also didn't know where it would explode. Andy had returned to South Block at about ten and was seated in a room with bare walls. Someone would consult him once in a while. In the afternoon, at about two, there was a sudden development. Andy was told that a doctor had been summoned to KB's house. He was flummoxed.

Andy requested permission to meet the doctor at the hospital. The approval letter from the Prime Minister's office allowed him through the numerous road blocks he encountered. By the time he reached there, the doctor had returned. He was a middle-aged man with bent shoulders, as if he was forever carrying the weight of his patients on them.

'What's the problem with KB sahib, doctor?'

He had, like most doctors, a permanent frown on his face. He looked at Andy through his thick shell glasses and said, 'Why should I tell you? Who are you?'

'I have the Prime Minister's authorization.' He produced the letter.

The doctor relaxed and sat down. His lips mumbled as Andy waited. It appeared as if he was making up his mind on how best to answer. Finally when he spoke his voice was uncertain. 'This might sound weird to you, but my best guess is he has been poisoned...maybe by...umm... nuclear radiation? But you know as much as I do, that this isn't a possibility!'

Andy agreed with him and said such a possibility was not feasible.

Then he thanked him and left, worried like hell. As he walked away from the hospital, he thought of the possible reasons for KB contracting radiation all of a sudden. KB was exposed and that could happen only if he was near the bomb. Probably the bomb got damaged while it was being transported to Delhi. He stiffened. KB was being watched and they were sure he had not left his house in the last 24 hours.

The bomb was in his house! This was a crucial finding.

Andy returned and met the NSA at once.

He had done a brief study. The unit for measurement

of nuclear radiation exposure is millisieverts. When some-one gets a CT scan done, the exposure is 20 millisieverts. Radiation sickness begins at exposure of over 1000 millisieverts. Medical complications and overall risk to human health increases with exposure.

'How much radiation did they detect at Murud?' Andy asked him.

'100, by the Geiger Counter.'

'That's quite safe. Going by those readings, we can use a Hazmat, or maybe a NBC suit.'

'What's better?' the NSA seemed edgy.

'Whatever we can lay our hands on faster. To the best of my knowledge, NBC suits are used only by the military, so we may not have them readily at New Delhi. But the police might have Hazmat suits.'

'We have NBC suits with the bomb squad of the NSG. It's about forty kilometres from here. I can get a few within the hour.' He seemed confident.

'OK, Sir.'

The NSA turned and said, his voice echoing as if it came back from a deep well, 'No one should be in the vicinity of the farm house. If a picture of our boys in NBC suits somehow reaches the media, it will spread mass panic amongst the people.'

Andy got into a waiting car and headed straight for

Chhatarpur. About half a kilometre short of KB's house, he was ushered into a covered truck. Andy greeted the Officer-in-Charge of the Bomb Squad. He was a young Captain. Twenty fit, battle-ready-soldiers looked at him with their focused, unwavering eyes. Though they didn't smile or respond to Andy's pleasantries, he knew from experience that they were ready.

'Captain Yash Singh,' the Officer-in-Charge shook Andy's hand confidently. He smiled, almost like he was all set for a party.

Andy liked his enthusiasm, something even he felt tingling in his bones, even after three years of having left the Army. The situation had, in a way, got him back into his old shoes.

'We have our orders, Sir. We will work as per your plan.'

Andy told him about his plan using a paper and a pen. His team had no doubts. Good soldiers seldom do.

The bomb squad had already brought several dozen specialized NBC suits that were suitable to work in areas with the risk of nuclear exposure. As per the plan, while Andy would enter the walled mansion from the rear, the bomb squad experts, in their NBC protective suits, would enter from the front. Once they had secured the outside, Andy would don the special suit too. With him in the lead, they decided to break into the house. They were expecting gunfire from both sides of the building.

Andy knew the enemy would be desperate. The circumstances now were such. With their leader unwell, their defences would be confused and weak.

Andy reached the rear end of KB's mansion and looked up at the imposing walls. He whistled to himself. The walls were about ten feet and appeared slippery. But he had come prepared —a rope and a grapnel anchor to tackle this eventuality. Delhi farmhouses have the tallest walls in the whole world and he knew that.

Andy threw the rope across the wall and pulled to check the grip. It held. He was aware of the risk and heard his heart thump in his chest. There could be gun fire even before he set foot inside the compound. But to ensure that the enemy's focus remained on the main entrance, he had included a frontal attack in his plan. Andy pulled out the walkie-talkie from his belt and gave the go ahead. It was all set.

After waiting for two minutes, he began to climb the wall. Once he was on the top, he rolled to the other side and lay on the grass. He could see a few armed men running towards the main gate, automatic weapons in their hands. They took shelter behind barricades made with sandbags. Andy passed their location to his team. He saw the gate partially open and a conversation take place. All seemed very quiet, like before a storm.

To create the convenient distraction, a helicopter appeared above them, the sounds from its blades closing as it descended lower and lower. Andy felt this completely unnecessary. It made him reassess the situation. Now the enemy was aware of an imminent attack. It was a bad decision.

He saw a man run from inside, his finger pointed up. Then the gates were closed and the men began firing blindly with their weapons in the direction of the helicopter. The sounds were menacingly close. The helicopter rose up and vanished. The men jumped and rejoiced. The incident had unnecessarily emboldened them.

Andy waited. Nothing happened. The men on other side of the gate held their ground. Captain Yash asked for the exact location of the people inside. Andy used his 3G phone and raised his hand slightly towards the gate. He quickly mailed them a picture, giving them the best possible scenario of the enemy inside the compound.

After a few seconds, he ordered for the gate to be blasted. As the gate was torn apart, Andy watched his team enter the farmhouse. The enemy had retracted inside. There were Ashoka trees planted in a line halfway between KB's house and the gate. They stopped there and waited for Andy to join them. Andy took the suit and put it on quickly.

They looked at him. Andy thought all of them looked like astronauts. He got his breathing rhythm in seconds as he adjusted to the breathing apparatus. They checked their communication through the in-built radio. It was all set.

21

They encircled the house from all the sides and began zeroing in. Slowly, one foot at a time, in coordination, all senses alert.

The silence was broken by a sudden burst of gun fire from inside. It came from a window that was on Andy's right. While he and the others gave cover by retaliating with quite bursts of fire, Captain Yash Singh ran on his haunches and reached under the window. The firing stopped from both the sides.

Andy nodded to Captain Yash who lobbed a grenade through the gap in the window. Seconds later they heard a loud explosion and the window panes blasted out, shards of glass falling a few feet from them. In no time, Andy and five soldiers ran towards the main door. Once they reached there, three each stood on either side, their backs pressed hard against the concrete.

This was the most difficult part. The enemy must have seen the soldiers drawing close and had chosen not to fire. The decision not to fire suggested that they had better control on their nerves — something that comes when you hold an ace up your sleeve.

A quick decision had to be made. This was not the time to contemplate. Andy had to divide the enemy's attention, shake their confidence a bit. He ordered an attack through one of the side windows. Captain Yash Singh led five more men inside.

Andy waited while they entered through the window. There was no sound. Captain Yash conveyed that the room was empty. As he said this, Andy heard a barrage of bullet fire. He heard shouts from Captain Yash's men. It seemed they had been surrounded and were being fired at indiscriminately.

As Andy charged inside with his team, he asked five more men from the waiting lot of soldiers to back Captain Yash's team through the window. Andy was fired at and a bullet tore through his suit near his thigh. He rolled on the floor and hid behind a large pillar. His men took the two people who fired at them. They crashed on the floor, but not before they had taken one of his soldiers. Andy pulled the injured soldier behind the pillar and asked for help from the back-up team. Then, leaving one of his soldiers behind with the injured, he charged inside in the direction he thought was the room where Captain Yash and his team were being fired at.

By the time he arrived the action was over. Captain Yash and his team stood over three dead men. They were wearing Pathani suits. Two soldiers had been injured on their side too. Captain Yash asked the medic to rush over at once.

'Let's break into three groups. It should be easy now,' he said. Everyone raised their thumbs in affirmation. Andy divided the team —he and Captain Yash leading four men each, and the last team led by a JCO.

They moved deeper into the house, clearing room after room. There were pictures of Hitler on the walls everywhere. Rare paintings, crystal figurines and ornate furniture made the house look like a museum. KB appeared to be a man of good taste, but greed had punctured his soul. Rich people always yearned for more money, while the poor just wanted enough to eat and provide for a roof over their heads. This is how the world had always existed, Andy though ruefully.

Blood from his wound was leaving a trail on the white tiled floor as he moved. It was not a good sign. He had no idea how many still remained on the enemy's side. Andy paused and took out a handkerchief. He tied it tightly over the wound and resumed his search. He knew he was losing blood and wondered if he should pull himself out of the battle to save his life. But he was trained to fight till his last breath, or until the enemy was conquered. At the moment the enemy was in hiding. His walking away could disillusion his men, though he had faith in Captain Yash. He decided to continue.

Outside he could hear the helicopters hovering closer. Reinforcements were on their way.

A single shot zipped past him and hit a soldier on his left. Andy dropped down on his knees. He heard feet running away, heavy sounds, like a giant man was trying to escape. He followed the sound and caught up with the man just as he was about to disappear beyond the other side of a long corridor. Andy fired a shot and the man stumbled and fell. He drew close, his pistol pointed at him. The man tried to turn around, but Andy fired once more. As Andy rushed up to him and got a good look at his face, he recognized him. He was the headstrong village buffoon Andy had met on his first day at Tilakpur.

The man was alive and tried to speak.

'I had told you that if you were the one who killed Ram Avtar, you were going to be in serious trouble.'

The man nodded and his head rolled over. He wanted to say something, but his lungs collapsed.

It took him another five minutes to locate KB's bedroom. With a pistol ahead of him and his hand resting firmly on the trigger, Andy pushed the door ajar and entered with caution.

The sight before him was something he had never expected. KB sat on a chair, his elbows resting on a large table. Andy looked around. There was no one else. A circular bed occupied the other side of the bedroom and a gargantuan glass chandelier towered over it from a very high ceiling.

KB was licking his palm that seemed covered in a white powdery substance. He knew what it was. Common salt. Andy knew consumption of iodized salt reduced the absorption of iodine from the air contaminated with nuclear radiation.

'So you haven't died?' KB's arrogance had not betrayed him yet. His face had turned excessively red and Andy could see the skin on his hands peeling off.

'No. But your time has come.' KB looked horrible.

'I won't die, the doctor has said I won't die.' He smiled at Andy. His face dripped evil all over.

'I can see that you are eating Indian salt, the salt of the same land you were about to betray.'

'Salt will protect me! Let's not talk about who is betraying whom.' He bent forward and vomited in a bucket on his side.

'Where is the bomb?'

Without any warning, KB suddenly got up and raised a pistol he was hiding behind his back. The adrenaline was still pumping and Andy didn't think twice. He aimed his gun right at the tottering old man and fired.

The monster collapsed like a gunny sack of sand thrown from a truck. The rotund body folded on itself. There was a suitcase on the table. Andy knew what its contents were.

He called Captain Yash and other members of his team to deal with the suitcase.

After fifteen minutes, Captain Yash stepped forward and said, 'Sir, the bomb is dead now, as much as that man there.' He pointed at KB.

The follow-up team had brought a lead box in which they kept the bomb, so as to contain further nuclear radiation. Then everyone moved out. The house and its surroundings had to be quarantined till the contamination tests were completed.

Outside the house, Andy met the NSA, Bhushan Singh. The old man hugged Andy and said, 'You are a true soldier... a soldier who risked his life to save the nation from such a huge embarrassment!'

Andy disagreed with him and replied, 'Every soldier is a true soldier. Only if you people in power knew of this basic fact.' He re-joined his team and they cheered and celebrated their win.

Andy returned home and slept. Peacefully. In the evening, he tuned into the television and the first thing he saw was the NSA. He was telling the nation how a well-coordinated operation was performed by the government with the help of intelligence agencies, state police and the National Security Guard. He flipped through channels and found other ministers also giving similar stories. No one took his name. He didn't expect them to. He felt good and alive, even as he missed Monica.

The next day, the NSA called Andy to his office in South Block. He had sent a car and Andy was chauffeured in style. When Andy reached his office, the man handed him a cheque of ten lakh rupees. That was all. Very business-like. He said he had a meeting to attend and Andy lied about getting somewhere fast himself. They shook hands and he was chauffeured back to his house.

EPILOGUE

Two days later, Andy drove down to Rewari. There was nothing to fear anymore. As he drove beyond Gurgaon, he noticed state transport buses carrying villagers with dazed expressions sitting in them, people he had travelled with in the not so distant past. He smiled and waved. They didn't respond and looked through him.

He confidently took the turn towards Tilakpur as it appeared. No one was expecting him there this time. He parked the car under the giant banyan tree, like he did the first time he visited. It was ten in the morning. The wind was strong and the chill made him shiver. He walked into the village and paused in front of Gulabo's door. He stood there for a while, before he finally knocked on the door.

The door swung open and a young girl stood there, looking at him quizzically. He had never seen Gulabo's daughter, though he could recognize it was her.

'Is this Ram Avtar's house?'

'Yes, but if you're here to ask for the money my father borrowed from you, I want to tell you that he never told us about his financial dealings.'

Andy smiled and took out the cheque he was carrying. He handed it to the girl and said, 'No, he didn't take any money from me. I did. Here, I hope this comes as some help to you.'

She accepted it, looking a bit uncertain. An older woman joined her. Andy could see the resemblance. Gulabo's daughter now lived with her grandmother and was finally safe.

The old lady looked at the cheque in the girl's hand.

'He says he had borrowed ten lakh rupees from Bauji. He has come to return it.'

The old woman looked at him in disbelief and said, 'He never told us anything about this. You are a good man.'

There was an uncertain pause and then she said, 'Please come in. Let me at least offer you a cup of tea...'

Andy declined her offer. 'I'm in a hurry,' he lied and started back as he heard the door close behind him. On the way to his car he saw the boy with two missing teeth, taking his buffaloes to the village pond.

They smiled and moved towards their respective destinations.

A week later, Andy was sitting at home, wondering what to do next when suddenly a phone call interrupted his thoughts.

'Hello! Is this Andy Karan?' It was a female voice he had never heard before.

'Yes.'

'Hi, I'm Angela. I'm the new managing editor at the *New Delhi Today* magazine. You're still working with us, aren't you?"

'Of course!' He didn't really know his status, but he lied nevertheless. After all, he had killed the mad owner of the magazine he worked for.

'OK, because with the ownership having changed hands I really wasn't sure.' The voice sounded professional.

'Well, I didn't technically resign... and neither was I fired.' Andy covered all his bases. His bank had intimated earlier in the morning that his balance was running low. His credit card payments were also steadily rising. He needed a job.

'Then could you please get here immediately. Something's come up in Goa and I think you're the best person to look into it.'

The first thing he realized after putting the phone down was that he was hungry. He peeled a banana and gobbled it in two bites. Then he quickly packed his survival kit: cell phone, laptop, wallet, chewing gums, a sweater, and a shaving kit, and Andy Karan was back in business.

Acknowledgements

The process of writing is lonely. Without the support of a faithful inner circle of friends and relatives, however talented and committed the writer is, in all probabilities, he will just wither away. Simple words of encouragement, occasional pat on the back, a candid feedback, or just hanging out with the writer, can go a long way in keeping him on track.

I have been lucky.

Thank you:

For encouragement & patience: Mom, Dad, Mom-in-law, Seema, Bunty, Vinita, Jeanie, Leah, Arnav and our extended family in Haryana and Delhi.

For support / mentoring: Tuhin Sinha, Iqbal Singh Chauhan, Shanti Perez, Andrew Bond, Rajeev Ranjan, Laxman Pangtey, Chandrayan Dey, N Somasundram, Sujata Parashar and Rakesh Sharma.

For remaining by my side: Sachin, Sanjay, Reema, Rachna, Ruhi, Liyasha, Vishal and Anu Jamwal, Rajeev Parashar, Satish Gupta and Amit Bhardwaj.

At Red Ink Literary Agency: Anuj Bahri, Sharvani Pandit, Subhojit Sanyal, Aanchal Malhotra, Sanya Sagar and Prerna Sodhi.